CAST OF C

Pat Montague. A recently discharged young Army lieutenant.

Helen Abbott Cairns. Pat's former sweetheart, now married to another.

Huntley Cairns. Her *nouveau riche* husband, a repugnant tub of a man.

Lawn Abbott. Helen's moody, headstrong younger sister.

Thurlow Abbott. Helen's father, a former musical comedy star.

Midge and Adele Beale. A happily quarrelsome couple. She was once romanced by Huntley Cairns.

Jed Nicolet. A young hotshot lawyer who respects Miss Withers.

Beulah and Jeff MacTavish. Servants to the Cairns. Don't be fooled by their thick plantation accents.

Bill Harcourt. A professional partygoer.

Harry Radebaugh. A young surgeon and acting deputy coroner.

Joe Searles. The Knowles' gardener, a disreputable old recluse.

Commander Sam Bennington. A retired Navy officer.

Albert Vinge. The local sheriff, who feels he's out of his depth here.

Mame and Trudy Boad. A society matron and her daughter.

Miss Hildegarde Withers. A prim, angular retired schoolteacher and tropical fish fancier, fond of meddling in murder.

Oscar Piper. A New York police inspector and longtime admirer of Miss Withers who alternately tolerates and is infuriated by her snooping.

Mr. Malone. A slick Cbicago lawyer.

Plus assorted neighbors, friends, and law enforcement officials.

Books by Stuart Palmer

Novels featuring Hildegarde Withers:
The Penguin Pool Murder (1931)
Murder on Wheels (1932)
Murder on the Blackboard (1932)
The Puzzle of the Pepper Tree (1933)
The Puzzle of the Silver Persian (1934)
The Puzzle of the Red Stallion (1936)
The Puzzle of the Blue Banderilla (1937)*
*The Puzzle of the Happy Hooligan (*1941)
Miss Withers Regrets (1947)*
Four Lost Ladies (1949)
The Green Ace (1950)
Nipped in the Bud (1951)*
Cold Poison (1954)
Hildegarde Withers Makes the Scene (1969)
(completed by Fletcher Flora)

*Reprinted by The Rue Morgue Press

Short story collections featuring Hildegarde Withers:
The Riddles of Hildegarde Withers (1947)
*The Monkey Murder (*1950)
People Vs. Withers and Malone (1963)
(with Craig Rice)
Hildegarde Withers: Uncollected Riddles (2003)

Howie Rook mysteries:
Unhappy Hooligan (1956)
Rook Takes Knight (1968)

Other mystery novels:
Ace of Jades (1931)
Omit Flowers (1937)
Before It's Too Late (1950)
(as by Jay Stewart)

Sherlock Holmes pastiches:
The Adventure of the Marked Man and One Other

Miss Withers
Regrets
by Stuart Palmer

Rue Morgue Press
Boulder / Lyons

To
Ann
with love

About Stuart Palmer

Stuart Palmer (1905-1968) referred to Hildegarde Withers as that "meddlesome old battleaxe" but he was as fond of her as were the readers and moviegoers of the 1930s. She debuted in 1931 in *The Penguin Pool Murder* where she met Inspector Oscar Piper of the New York Homicide Squad. Set in 1929 shortly after the collapse of the stock market, *The Penguin Pool Murder* was filmed a year later with Edna May Oliver as Miss Withers and James Gleason as Oscar Piper. The lighthearted movie became one RKO's biggest hits of the year. Oliver was perfect in the role, perhaps because Palmer was inspired to create Miss Withers after seeing Oliver on stage during the first run of Jerome Kern's *Showboat*, although he also used other people from his past to round off her character, including a librarian from his home town of Baraboo, Wisconsin, who disapproved of his literary tastes, and a "horse-faced English teacher" from his high school days. He credited his father as the inspiration for Miss Withers' Yankee sense of humor.

Miss Withers appeared in eight novels between 1931 and 1941 and then went on sabbatical for six years while her creator labored in Hollywood where he eventually wrote 37 scripts, including several in the Falcon and Bulldog Drummond series. In 1944 at nearly the age of 40 he enlisted in the army and was sent to Oklahoma where he produced training films on field artillery. In 1947, Palmer revisited Miss Withers in *Miss Withers Regrets* and went on to produce four more books in this series during the early 1950s. The last Withers novel, *Hildegarde Withers Makes the Scene*, was completed by Fletcher Flora after Palmer's death in 1968. Jennifer Venola, Palmer's fifth wife, whom he married when he was 60 and she just 21, called his death a "rational suicide" following a diagnosis of terminal laryngeal cancer. At his wish, his body was donated to the Loma Linda Medical School for study.

For more information on Stuart Palmer see Tom and Enid Schantz' introduction to The Rue Morgue Press edition of *The Puzzle of the Blue Banderilla*.

Warning to the reader:

Some of you may be upset to encounter some stereotypical dialog on the part of some of the black characters in this book and put it down to the racial attitudes of the times. Be advised that this is not the case. The patient reader will soon discover that the very funny Mr. Palmer may well have been ahead of his times. The wise reader will also encounter a character "borrowed" from the work of another mystery writer. We wouldn't dream of spoiling that surprise.

CHAPTER ONE

Far off there was thunder, in spite of the summer sunshine which blazed down on the solitary young man who walked along the curving highway. Thunder on the left, Pat Montague thought, was supposed in the Greek tragedies to portend significant and marvelous events. Or maybe this was simply more Navy maneuvers, except that they wouldn't be apt to hold forth in Long Island Sound.

Ahead of him in the roadway there danced a little whirlpool, a midget tornado of dead leaves and dust. The pixie thing spun wildly, swooped and lifted and fell again, and finally went pirouetting off across the green slopes towards the trees.

Pat kept on walking; not that he had to walk. There was a fat wad of mustering-out pay in his pocket, and he could have taken a taxi. It was only that he felt more at home afoot, having just unpinned the crossed muskets of the infantry. Walking gave him more time to think, more time to brood about the clipping in his billfold. He had carefully extracted it from the society column of an Oyster Bay newspaper, where he had found it only by the purest accident only a few days ago, and it was already almost worn out.

Too, walking gave him more chance to change his mind. Until he had actually committed himself by ringing the doorbell he could turn around at any moment and head back to town, pretending that he had just been out for a stroll in the fresh air, practicing at being a civilian. He wasn't at all sure that he was going to ring that doorbell, because when he tried to think about Helen his mind went round and round like the dust whirlpool and settled nowhere.

Men without women, men forced into the unnaturally monastic routines of training camps and troop carriers, usually had tried to stop thinking about the opposite sex. The pinup girls with their exaggerated curves of breast and leg were taken down after the first month or two. But Helen's picture had been with him always, because it had been printed on his mind at sunrise one morning in what seemed to be indelible colors.

He had even found himself talking to that picture sometimes. That was the way things got out of proportion, and the line between actual memory and daydreams became indistinct. He could remember long conversations with Helen, but whether they occurred when they were together or during the three long years between, he couldn't have sworn.

Somehow it wasn't as easy being Mr. Montague again as he had thought. The Army had spent a few days cramming him with rehabilitation, teaching him how to be a civilian. The dull and unpleasant overseas camping trip which he had been forced to make, in company with some millions of other healthy, bored young men, was finished and done for. There wasn't a stitch of government-issue clothing on his body, and he had even bought a new billfold, a new penknife. But he sensed that it was going to take more than that.

Anyway, he was free again, and his legs were moving out of cadence. Even the weather was mixed up in his mood. On a fresh, gusty afternoon like this, with warm sunshine pouring down and yet with squalls over the Sound, it wasn't hard for a young man to convince himself that the whole world loves a lover and that things are bound to come right in the end.

Even though the girl was married. The newspaper clipping had forcibly reminded him of that. "… Mrs. Cairns, the former Helen Virginia Abbott of New York City and …"

But that was quite in the classical tradition too, Pat reminded himself. The other Helen had been married to some meatball named Menelaus. So had Guinevere, and Isolde, and Balkis Queen of Sheba, and Deirdre, and Scarlett O'Hara.

All, all married, to men they didn't love. Each waiting for the lover to come along.

So it was that with a quick-frozen dream in his heart and a large chip on his shoulder Pat Montague marched along an elm-shaded roadway in a very expensive section of Long Island, drawn by the most powerful magnetic force known to mankind. He walked, without realizing it, almost in the center of the road and was very nearly clipped off at the pockets by a small convertible roadster which came roaring around the curve behind him. It was a very close thing for a fraction of a second, and then Pat flung himself towards the edge of the road and safety.

The little car swerved and went rocketing by, its horn blatting furiously. Pat swore with the easy profanity of the soldier, but it was more at himself than at the driver. She had looked like a remarkably pretty girl. Maybe if that little man hadn't been sitting beside her she'd have stopped and offered him a ride. People were apt to do that nowadays, even if you weren't still wearing the uniform.

Pat began to wonder if he was developing a blister on his right heel. The new black shoes—he had sworn never to wear brown again—were lighter in weight than the ones he was used to. Also, it seemed to be farther to the Cairns place than he had imagined it would be, with more uphill to it.

Then he came around a turn and saw the salmon-colored house silhouetted against the Sound, big and new and imposing. Pat knew without a moment's hesitation that this was the right place, because only Huntley Cairns would create a thing like this, half Riviera villa and half Los Angeles Moorish.

Snatches of South American dance music drifted back to him, and Pat began to breathe a little faster. He rehearsed again what he was going to do and what he was going to say. He had it pretty well worked out if it happened to be Cairns himself who came to the door. He would say, "Well, Fatso! *Still* leading with your right?"

More probably it would be a servant. In that case he would give out with his best smile and say, "I'm Pat Montague, an old friend of the family."

But if Helen herself came to the door …

Surprisingly enough, Pat found his long legs carrying him right past the gateway of the new house and on along the crest of the hill. After a little way his stride shortened, and finally he stopped for breath. He climbed upon the tree bank so he could look down on the place. There must have been ten acres of it, maybe more if it ran all the way down to the shore. It was all terraced and landscaped and set with the proper shrubbery, and what ancient trees had been allowed to remain were all neatly pruned and trimmed and daubed around the trunk with white stickum.

Huntley Cairns, after raising that pastry cook's dream of a house, couldn't have waited for anything to grow. It all had the dreadful impermanence of things which are too new and perfect and shining.

Pat could see nothing of Helen's personality anywhere, nothing that could have been her choice. That made it easier, somehow. She didn't belong here; she didn't belong in Fatso Cairns's house, or in his arms.

There was a barrier fence of split logs bright with whitewash, and beyond that the green lawns sloped away, studded with round flower gardens, littered with rustic benches and pebbled walks. From where he was standing he could see the side of the house and one end of a balcony. To the rear of the house the ground sloped down more sharply to the garage and toolshed, beyond them a smaller white building.

Farther still was the glimmer of green-blue water. Pat walked on a few steps so that he could see, between the buildings, a narrow glimpse of an oval swimming pool bordered with bright-colored tiles. The sun disappeared now and there was a spatter of rain, but Pat Montague did not notice it.

Beside the pool, which must have been a good quarter of a mile away from where he stood, there was the flash of white, which disappeared immediately. Pat forgot to breathe as he realized who it must be. He started to climb the fence, the blood pounding in his temples. As long as he had known her, Helen's bathing suits had always been white.

His guardian angel looked the other way, and there was laughter in hell as Pat Montague walked slowly down across the grass, threading his way along the terraces, around the flower gardens and the rustic benches, and at last came around the corner of the little white bathhouse which overlooked the pool. He stopped then, and went on more slowly.

There was nobody here, nobody at all. He wondered if he had been seeing things, if his imagination had been playing him tricks again. The swimming pool was a peaceful turquoise green, troubled only by the sprinkle of rain and by the little chill wind which was rolling up from the sound.

A shadow flitted by him, and Pat looked up to see a brown hawk wheeling overhead, whistling and watching.

Then a disreputable station wagon pulled into the service driveway and stopped, with a rattling gasp and a final rattle of buckets, tools, and patched garden hose. From it, after a moment, emerged a wiry, spare man of about sixty, clad in filthy blue overalls, with a sack of manure on his shoulder.

He looked towards the pool, dropped the sack, and started hurrying. Pat Montague, kneeling beside the pool, heard the sound of feet and looked up, his face gray and pasty. He had been prodding down into the water with a garden rake.

"Lose something, mister?"

Pat did not answer, and the old man came closer, squinting with moist and bloodshot eyes down into the greenish depths at the deep end of the

pool, under the diving board. Staring back at him was the round white
face of his employer, Huntley Cairns, under two fathoms of carefully
warmed and heavily chlorinated water.

Somehow the two men raked and tumbled the body out on to the tiles.
It was dressed in some weird and outlandish garment which seemed to be
a combination corset and underdrawers, stiff with stays and tight elastic.
Pat whispered through stiff lips: "He may not be dead. We could try first
aid. Sometimes you can bring them back—"

The old man shook his head brusquely. His cracked, thin voice was
commanding. "Never mind that," he ordered. "You get in there and phone
for an ambulance, do you hear?" He was pointing to the open door of a
dressing room in the white bathhouse behind them.

If there was anything odd about the old man, except for his smell, Pat
didn't notice it then. It seemed to him the most natural thing in the world
to follow orders. He rose and ran obediently into a long bare room with a
shower at the far end, a room which he vaguely noticed was furnished
with wooden benches and wall hooks, presumably meant to be used by
the masculine guests of the household. A couple of bathing trunks hung
on the hooks, a towel and a wet suit lay in a puddle on the concrete floor,
and a bathrobe and some men's clothing were spread out neatly on a
bench.

The extension telephone hung on the rear wall, near the shower. Pat
grabbed the receiver, jiggled the hook feverishly, and then heard the door
slam shut behind him. It wasn't the wind, either, because a second later
there was the definite, final sound of a key being turned in the lock.

Even then Pat didn't have the slightest idea of what was happening, or
of the trap into which he had walked so willingly. He peered out of the
one window, which was placed so that it gave only a glimpse of whitish-
gray sky. The door was securely locked; he made sure of that. Dazed, he
went back to the telephone again, but when he put the instrument to his
ear he could hear the cracked, excited voice of the gardener. "… yes,
Searles! I work days for Mr. Cairns. I said he was *murdered*—I caught a
young fellow in the act, I tell you!"

The voice at the other end of the line was masculine and calm.
"Somebody'll be right out there. Can you keep him?"

"Sure, sure. I got him all right! But make it snappy."

Pat stood there, a foolish, frozen grin on his face. He watched a daddy-
long-legs doing acrobatics up the side of the wall. And then the impact
struck him, a delayed-action bomb going off in his head.

It was he—Pat Montague—they were talking about!

He turned and threw himself breathlessly at the locked door. In spite of the fact that his technique was exactly the same as he had always seen in the movies, nothing happened. His shoulder began to throb numbly. He backed up, took a deep breath, and prepared to try again.

Then he suddenly froze in what must have been an exceptionally ridiculous position as the lock clicked. Light struck him in the face, and he saw that a girl stood there, silhouetted against the stormy sky. It was a girl whom Pat had not seen for years and would have been very happy never to have seen again.

Lawn, Lawn Abbott. Helen's changeling kid sister, the queer coltish girl who always used to go around in a cowboy shirt, with blue jeans turned up almost to her bony knees and moccasins on her feet. Now she wore riding clothes, jodhpurs, which flattered her straight, almost feral young body. They were soiled and wet, and she held a light thin riding crop with a silver knob on the top.

The face which looked so blankly into Pat's was cool and aloof as always, the scornful lower lip glistening red. She bit a fingernail thoughtfully.

Of all people to find him here, Pat thought bitterly, it would have to be Lawn, who had always hated him and done her level best to spoil his romance with her sister! He swallowed. This was all the bad luck in the world rolled up into a lump.

What made it more *fubar* than anything was the fact that he had never been able to reach her, to talk to her at all. She had always slipped away like quicksilver, a strange, medieval girl who looked right through him. But he had to talk to her now. He had to make her see what it would mean to Helen if he were caught here like this, with Cairns lying dead on the tiles.

Pat started making explanations, which really didn't explain at all. But the girl just stared at him, the dark eyes—so like Helen's but without her dream-weighted innocence—making a time exposure. Her eyebrows, the V-shaped, satanic eyebrows, were barely lifted. In some odd feline way she seemed to be enjoying this moment, savoring it to its last essence. Finally he ran down, not that he hadn't more to say, but only because no sign of warmth or understanding lighted that bloodless Medici mask of a face.

Then she suddenly caught his hands in her hard, small brown ones, pulled him through the door, and thrust him down the hill, away from the house. Her voice was throaty, a deep contralto, and she spoke as though to a not-very-bright child.

"That way! Keep where you can't be seen from the house. There's the path I take to the stables, only you cut left just before you get to the shore. You'll come out on the third tee of the golf course, and then keep right. The village is about a mile and a half."

Pat tried to mutter something, but she caught him short, almost shoving him along as if possessed by some deep inner rage.

He started running, not pausing until he reached the shadow of the trees far below. Then he looked back and saw that Lawn Abbott was gingerly lifting the coat which the gardener had flung over the body of her brother-in-law. She didn't look up or turn, but her hand gestured him impatiently on. The music from the big house continued, very softly, where someone was playing that most mournful of tangos: "*Adios muchachos, compañeros, de ma vida ...*"

Pat turned and went on. Then, above the music and the hushing sound of the rain in the elms, he heard for the first time the faraway wolf call of the police sirens. It was a hunting call, and they were hunting him.

CHAPTER TWO

"I suppose that was my fault!" the thin pretty girl at the wheel of the convertible exploded, turning towards her husband. Midge Beale shrugged his hard, narrow shoulders. He was always nervous about Adele's driving, mostly because he felt a deep though mute kinship with motors. She was always handling machinery as if she were angry at it, and a little contemptuous too, like a girl from the wrong side of the tracks suddenly made mistress of a big house and too many servants.

"You'd better stop," he told her.

"Why should I stop, for heaven's sake? I didn't actually hit him, did I? And if you think I'm going to pick up every hitchhiker on the road …" Adele's wide, thin-lipped mouth tightened under its generous layer of geranium lipstick, and she tossed her fluffy brown hair like an annoyed horse. "Probably just another discharged veteran thinking he's entitled to free transportation."

They swung around another corner and came out on the crest of the hill, leaving the elm trees and their shade behind. Spread out before them was a vast panorama of water and sky, with white fleecy clouds scudding along and a great thunderhead moving north towards Connecticut. Two sailboats, under light canvas, were beating their way around the point.

"I only suggested stopping back there because I thought I recognized that fellow you almost hit," Midge said slowly.

His wife stared at him. "You mean somebody from the field?"

"No, my love. I thought he looked a lot like old Pat Montague."

Adele's mouth opened wide. "Pat? But he's overseas in Germany or Austria or somewhere."

"It may come as a great surprise to you," Midge told her, "but they are even letting lieutenants out of the Army now."

Adele thought about that, biting her lower lip with very white but somewhat prominent front teeth. "You're probably just imagining things, darling. And if by some fantastic trick of fate it was really Pat, I'm certainly glad we didn't stop. Do you think I'd want to appear at Helen Cairns's housewarming with her old heart-throb in tow? That would be just a little too-too!"

Midge pointed out reasonably that he hadn't wanted to appear at all. "If we really have to get drunk, why can't we do it quietly at home?"

"Don't be stuffy, darling," Adele snapped. "Nowadays you can still dislike a man and drink his liquor. Otherwise our social life would be pretty limited, wouldn't it? You're certainly not jealous of Huntley, after all these years! Besides, he has a lot of connections, and he could help in getting you a different job."

"There's too much night work, working in the black market!"

"Oh, stop repeating gossip! Just because a man manages to get materials to build a new house and happens to get a new car before the rest of us …" Adele smiled. "Besides, Huntley is in some sort of public-relations work. Anyway, I was at Miss Prescott's with Helen, and she's a dear girl if you like that sleepy, almost bovine type. I couldn't resist a chance to see her new house, could I? Helen always had no taste at all in decoration. I remember her room at school was just a hodgepodge of family pictures and sentimental souvenirs. I can't wait to see the inside of the place."

The outside of the place, salmon-pink and imposing, suddenly presented itself around a turn in the drive, and Adele hit the brakes sharply before turning in through the gateway. "Now, darling," she begged, "for the love of heaven, don't go shooting off your mouth as soon as we get inside. I mean about your wild idea that you saw Pat Montague. It probably wasn't him at all but just somebody who looked like him."

Midge promised. He was forcibly reminded of that promise a few minutes later, when as he was still nursing his first martini he heard his wife's clear, brittle voice from the other end of the long, bare, functional-moderne drawing room. She was trilling at their hostess: "Helen, my dear! Just guess if you can who Midge thought he saw today right here in Shoreham! Give up? It was Pat, Helen, Pat Montague!"

Helen took it without even batting her wide, sleepy aquamarine eyes. Her beautiful, almost too-tranquil face blossomed into a smile, the little-girl smile that always started with a twist of her mouth. "Really? Dear old Pat. How was he looking? Was he still in uniform or—"

Then, without waiting for an answer, Helen picked up the martini mixer and refilled somebody's glass, which really didn't need it at all. With the greatest of poise she proceeded to set the massive crystal cylinder down on thin air about six inches from the edge of the blond-mahogany coffee table.

After the deluge it was of course Adele who sounded off with the first "Ohs" of sympathy. Across the room her husband looked at her dispassionately and wondered how it would feel to take that thin white neck in his hands and twist it. Just because of things like this.

But somehow the moment passed. The party wasn't well under way as yet, and Adele and Midge were the only people here who had known Helen when she was Helen Abbott, the only ones who realized how Pat had once fitted into the picture.

They—and Thurlow Abbott, of course. But her father didn't count; he hadn't counted very much since the days when bootleg gin had done something to his vocal cords, ending his career as a matinee-idol tenor in musical comedy. At this moment he was down on his creaky though well-tailored knees, trying to be helpful and mopping at his daughter's lime-green hostess gown with a napkin coyly printed in silver "Helen and Huntley."

Adele moved away, and Midge came up quickly behind her. "That was a nice fox pass," he said in a low voice. "All I can say, it's a good thing Cairns isn't here yet."

"I found out, anyway," Adele murmured, half to herself. But she wouldn't tell him what.

Somebody at the canape table said that their host had been kept late at the office and would be out on the five-o'clock. Meanwhile, with Helen swiftly disappearing upstairs to do something about another gown and some different eyeshadow, the guests rearranged themselves, scattering through the vastness of the lower floor and the paved patio outside. Midge stood aloof for a few minutes, like a man on a springboard looking down dubiously into troubled waters.

A handsome, coffee-colored youth in a white jacket went by, and he hailed him. "Martinis?"

"Yassuh! With olive or without olive?"

"Nope, no olives. Can't stand 'em. I want mine without onion."

The boy laughed politely.

"That wasn't so very funny," Midge said.

"Nossuh," agreed the boy. He moved away, but Midge managed to grab a glass.

"And to think that I used to enjoy these rat races," he said to himself. Then his eyes brightened as he saw a pair of incredibly luscious twins across the room, duplicate pinup girls come alive. Probably models, Midge thought. If he went over and paid court to them Adele would froth at the mouth for a week. Besides, they were a couple of inches taller than Midge was. It would also, he thought, be quite a job to get them separated.

Adele herself had clamped her hooks on to Harry Radebaugh, the dark-eyed, prematurely gray young surgeon who'd opened his own clinic in the village and had made so much money the first two years that he'd bought the old Bailey house and remodeled it. She was probably, Midge decided, entertaining him with an account of her insomnia. But she had eyes in the back of her head; he knew that from bitter experience. The twins wouldn't be worth it.

He went over to the table again and made a Dagwood special for himself out of caviar, cream cheese with chives, sausage, and an oyster. It would probably be all the dinner he would get.

Then he looked up to see his host, Huntley Cairns, come hurrying into the room through the front doors. He was apologizing right and left, which was typical. Cairns was the sort of man who was always begging you to forgive him for shaking your hand while wearing a glove, or because the big car was laid up and he had to take you to the village in the station wagon, or because there wasn't any cognac, there was only Scotch and bourbon.

"Sorry I'm so late, but better late than never," Cairns was saying. "Been working like a dog all day and I'm dirty as a pig. Drink up, everybody, and I'll be back as soon as I get cleaned up."

He was a little man, broad in the beam, with the breast pocket of his neat pinstripe blue suit crammed with gold pens and pencils. "Bet he comes down togged out in something sharp and two-toned, probably with suede shoes," Midge said to himself.

He must have said it aloud, for someone beside him asked, "What's that?"

It was Bill Harcourt, a large cheery man who was apt to tell hairy-dog stories on the third drink and pass out on the fourth. He lived, so far as any one could tell, on the food and drink he picked up at parties, which he could scent ten miles off, and on memories of his family's pre-1929 money.

"Hi," Midge said. "Just talking to myself."

Harcourt nodded blankly. "How's it by you? Still grounded?"

"They let me go up in elevators now," Midge confided, and looked towards the stairs. Huntley Cairns was turning to the right at the landing.

It must be true, then, that he and Helen had separate bedrooms—separate suites, even, for she had turned to the left when she rushed up to change.

Midge felt suddenly sorry for his host. Money wouldn't buy everything, at that. Of course it would buy more than pants buttons would, which was about all he would have if the plant finally closed down. Test pilots rarely saved a good deal of money, especially test pilots with nothing to test and given a courtesy job fiddling around with blueprints and T squares.

"I should have taken the job with Howard Hughes when I had a chance," Midge decided "Then when production slacked off I could go out and help put up three-sheets of movie stars' bosoms." He laughed, and realized that he was laughing all by himself. Looking over the crowd, he decided he would just as soon stay by himself. He could see Ava Bennington trying to catch his eye, but he was allergic to Navy wives, especially when their husbands were ashore. Besides, whenever he was near her he found it difficult to resist the temptation to ask her if the old tradition was true—about call-house madams saving up their profits so they could retire and marry Annapolis men.

Midge deftly managed to avoid her and then nearly ran into mountainous old Mame Boad, who owned half the village, including the house he rented. She sported a string of yellow pearls as large as .38 bullets around her wattled neck, and the reddish-brown dress she wore made her look exactly like a turkey. Her daughter Trudy, long in the tooth and very freckled, was close behind her. According to rumor, she was not allowed to smoke or drink yet, though she must be nearly thirty. This, Midge felt, called for a strategic withdrawal.

He withdrew, heading out on to the patio, but there was a sprinkle of rain and he came back, to become involved in the little circle around Colonel Wyatt, a fierce old eagle of a man who had guessed wrong about the military ability of both the Japanese and the Russians, and whose life had become embittered thereby.

Midge ricocheted off the edge of this gathering and finally found a haven in the library, a long narrow room lined almost to the ceiling with books. There was a desk at one end and a large fireplace faced by a divan at the other. The cushions were stuffed with real down, and Midge Beale sank into them with a deep gratefulness of spirit.

There had been absolutely no intention on his part to doze off, as he swore later. He intended only to close his eyes for a few moments to rest them from the glare and the smoke. But he jerked wide awake some time later, to hear voices nearby. It took a minute or two for him to orient himself—and then he stiffened, keeping down well behind the back of the divan.

"… and it could be a blind," said somebody in a hushed, male voice. "Cairns is foxier than he looks."

"Nonsense. Look, here's *The Dark Gentleman, Beautiful Joe*, and two Terhune's collie stories. " That was a voice Midge recognized, that of Jed Nicolet, a hotshot lawyer with offices in the Empire State, who always spent his summers out here in a big house half a mile down the road that hadn't been changed in thirty years.

For some reason the two men were cataloguing Cairns's library. Midge wished they would go away and let him sleep.

"He could have let somebody else pick 'em out. Not his wife—I don't think Helen ever reads anything except maybe the ads in *Vogue*. But her sister—"

"I can speak for her," Nicolet said. "Lawn Abbott doesn't read anything except modern poetry. By the way I wish she'd show up. There's a girl who—" He stopped short. "Say, look here, Bennington! Listen to this—the book just fell open!"

Bennington. That would be Ava's husband, Commander Sam Bennington, who'd retired from the Navy six months ago to sit on his big behind and help spend Ava's money. He was still talking. "Or he could have ordered his books by the linear foot, to match the color scheme."

"Sam, I said look here!" There was something in Jed Nicolet's voice so compelling that Midge couldn't resist poking his head up above the back of the divan. Both men were eagerly bent over a slender red volume which Nicolet had taken from a case near where he stood at the far end of the room. The young lawyer's fox face was alight with eagerness. "Listen to this!"

"Wait!" Bennington suddenly said. He turned and started towards the divan. Behind him Jed Nicolet hastily whipped the book back into the shelves again. Then he, too, converged on Midge.

"Spying on us, eh?" Bennington growled unpleasantly. "Get up!"

Midge started to rise and then sank quickly back again. "Oh, no," he retorted. "I don't bite on that one."

"You sneaking little eavesdropper—"

"How do you make that out? I was here first."

"Take it easy, Sam," Jed Nicolet put in. "Look, Beale, this is a little awkward. We didn't know you were here."

"That goes double. I didn't even expect to see you at this party, not after the trouble you had with Cairns."

Nicolet hesitated. "Sure, why not? After all, Helen is—well, she's Helen. And Lawn is a very good friend of mine. After all, why hold a grudge? The vet did pull Wotan through. He limps a little on one leg, that's all. Spoils him for show. But I thought it over and I realized that Cairns may not have seen him after all—a black Dane on a dark night. I decided this is too small a town to hold a grudge in."

Commander Bennington snorted. "I still say a man should know if he ran his car smack into a two-hundred-pound dog. But never mind that. Look, Beale. About what we were talking about—"

"I didn't hear a thing," Midge hastily assured them. And then the tension was broken by the booming voice of Mame Boad as she swept in upon them through the doorway.

"Well, what did you find?" she demanded breathlessly. "I'm so impatient that I—" She stopped short as she saw their expressions.

"We were just talking about things," Nicolet admitted.

"And that reminds me," Mrs. Boad cried. "This is a charming house Huntley Cairns has thrown together, all full of gadgets and cute as a bug's ear. I like it, even if I do miss the nice old-fashioned place that used to stand here. But what this house needs is the patter of little feet, and I mean paws. Next litter of pups my bitch has, I'm going to make Huntley buy one for Helen." Here she cocked a quizzical eye. "Or doesn't our host *like* dogs?"

"The question before the court," Jed Nicolet told her, "is how young Beale feels about them."

Mame Boad blinked. "Oh, for heaven's sake! Don't mind him. He looks to me like a man who's just crazy about dogs."

They all looked at Midge. "Well, in a way I am," he admitted. "Only the doctors said that my asthma was caused by dog hairs, so I—" He gulped. "What's everybody so serious for, anyway? Will it be okay if I buy a Mexican hairless?"

Bennington's face, weathered by years of salt winds and alcohol fumes, was redder than usual now. "Look here, Beale, since you know this much you might as well—"

It was Helen's cool, sweet voice which interrupted them this time. "So here you all are! My very nicest guests, hiding out from the party!" Jed Nicolet moved forward, but she patted his shoulder in passing and took Midge's arm in hers. "Come with me, young man. Don't be so elusive— Leilani Linton is just dying to dance with you, and we've got a lot of new rumba and samba records." She was smiling, but there was something strange and set in her smile, as if she had turned it on and couldn't find the switch to turn it off.

So Midge gladly suffered himself to be led along. Nor was he very surprised to find that neither Leilani nor Aloha Linton happened to be anywhere in sight and that it was Helen herself who wanted to dance with him. She even kicked off her shoes so that she was on his level.

But instead of taking the position for the rumba, she came breathtakingly close into his arms, the lush perfection of her body and the scent in her hair making his knees suddenly turn to rubber. Her lovely face was flushed, and he would have thought her a bit tight except that he hadn't seen her take even one drink.

Helen didn't want to dance either. She simply wanted to ask him something. It took them one turn around the room before he could guess, because she barely hinted at the thing that was on her mind.

"Oh!" Midge said. "Well, of course I'm not at all sure that it was Pat. He looked a little taller and straighter, but that could be the Army. I just had a quick glimpse of his face as we came past. You know how Adele drives."

"You—you came *past?*" she breathed in his ear.

"Oh, yes," he admitted. "About halfway up the hill. Pat, or whoever it was, seemed headed this way."

For a moment she stiffened, and then sagged so that he held almost all her weight in his arms. "Look, Helen," he whispered. "Is anything wrong? I mean is there anything I can do?"

"You can get me a drink," she said, but when he came back with a double martini in each hand she was gone. He looked for her vainly in the drawing room, in the playroom, in the dining room and hall, and finally downed both drinks, for economy's sake. A pleasantly pink fog began to close in upon him at that point. He had memories later of trying to play ping-pong with Trudy Boad and of losing the ball somewhere and of looking for Adele and not being able to find her either.

When the fog lifted again he was somehow in the kitchen, that wonderful Flash Gordon kitchen with the automatic everything and the glass-walled stove and refrigerator, drinking milk out of a quart bottle and singing with Bill Harcourt, Doc Radebaugh, and the houseboy, whose name was Jeff and who had a fine deep contrabass.

> *"We'll serenade our Louie*
> *While life and love shall last ..."*

A dirty old man in overalls was screaming at them to shut up so he could use the kitchen telephone, and the quartet moved into the serving pantry. But even there, just as they were going good with "Oh, a Man without a Woman," they were suddenly silenced by the screaming of the police sirens.

"The party's a success!" Bill Harcourt cried. "It's a raid—don't give your right names!"

Then Lawn Abbott, her face whiter than ever, came inside to tell them what was lying at the edge of the swimming pool.

CHAPTER THREE

For a house whose every window blazed with light, the Cairns place was strangely quiet. The radio-phonograph was stilled, with a needle stuck in the middle of a record. Dishes and glasses were piled sticky and unwashed in the kitchen sink, unwiped ashtrays slowly overflowed on to the table-tops and rugs, and out on the service porch there was nobody to hear the soft drip-drop of the water which seeped from the body of Huntley Cairns and ran off into a bed of young hyacinths.

Then Officer Ray Lunney tapped on the front door, then looked in and beckoned to Sergeant Fischer, who immediately joined him outside. "Sheriff's coming," Lunney said. "I can hear that heap of his gasping up the hill."

"About time he got here," pointed out Fischer complacently. "We're ready for him. You know old man Vinge, if he gets the idea there's any complicated angles to a case, he's apt to sidestep. He's not going to risk making any enemies, especially in this touchy section, with him having to stand for election every two years. You go inside and keep everybody quiet while I give him the lowdown."

Sergeant Fischer waited until Lunney was inside and then turned and headed out into the driveway. The Sheriff's conservative black sedan coughed its way up the hill and turned into the driveway, and then a fatherly-looking man started to get out, peering through thick-lensed glasses.

"We're taking bows tonight, Sheriff," Fischer said cheerily. "The case is all washed up and put to bed. We've got our man tied up in the back seat of the radio car, all ready to take into town. He's guilty as a skunk in a chicken yard."

Sheriff Vinge nodded a little uncomfortably. "Good, good. Er—who is it?"

"Don't worry," the sergeant assured him. "It's nobody—I mean it's only Joe Searles. You know, the old codger that drives around in an old station wagon loaded with junk, talking to himself half the time."

Vinge began to relax. "Oh! Yeah, I know him. Lives alone in a shack down by the wharf. Why'd he do it?"

"There wasn't any actual quarrel that we can prove," Fischer explained. "But it's only natural that the old man would have a grudge against a man like Cairns, who made a lot of money overnight and bought this place. The house that used to stand here, you know, was originally built by Joe Searles's own grandfather. He owned all the land along here once—used to grow hops and sorghum. I don't guess Searles has ever got over the idea that it's rightly his. The old man's done plenty of talking around the village, too. About how he didn't like Cairns, and how Cairns didn't know anything about trees or flowers or how to take care of land. And Cairns seems to have complained about the size of the bills old man Searles was running up at the nursery and the feed store. There was bad blood be-tween 'em, Sheriff, and I don't think Searles will hold out for more'n two or three hours of questioning."

"That makes sense," the sheriff said, definitely happier now. "Go on."

"Well, it figures like this. Searles had been so grouchy around the place that Mrs. Cairns—that's the pretty, plump girl who used to be Helen Ab-bott when she came out here summers—she sent him off on some er-rands, to buy fertilizer and stuff, so he wouldn't be around growling at the guests during the party if they walked on a tulip bed or picked a rose or something. Only he came back early, and he saw Cairns splashing around in the swimming pool. On a homicidal impulse he took a garden rake and held him under, right against the bottom of the pool. When he was sure Cairns was through breathing he dragged the body out and then rushed to phone us a crazy story about how he saw somebody else doing it. He claims he locked this guy—the usual tall dark powerful stranger—in the men's side of the bathhouse down there, but of course when we unlocked it there was nothing inside but some of Mr. Cairns's clothes."

Sheriff Vinge nodded. "No witnesses?"

"There wouldn't be any, Sheriff. It was sprinkling a little, and that kept the guests inside. Lawn Abbott—that's Mrs. Cairns's younger sister—came up the hill past the pool a few minutes after Searles rushed into the house to phone us, but she was too late to see him at work, which was no doubt lucky for her."

"Guess so. Well, as long as I'm here I may as well look at the body."

"On the service porch. I'll show you." Sergeant Fischer snapped on his electric torch and led the way around the house. "We brought it up here where the light was better so Doc Radebaugh could make his examination. Don't suppose there was any harm moving him, as long as he'd been moved once already."

"I got no objection, anyway," said the sheriff dryly. "And I don't guess Cairns has." He looked down upon the uncovered body of Huntley Cairns. "Good God, what's that thing he's got on?"

"An athletic corset, the doc called it. To keep his stomach in."

Vinge shook his head. "Bet you it was uncomfortable." He turned away. "Funny thing Searles would pull the body out of the water before he phoned. And, by the way, where'd he phone from?"

"He came up to the kitchen. That's one of the ways we trapped him, because he could just as well have phoned from the extension down in the bathhouse."

"But according to his story, he had the murderer locked in there, didn't he?"

"In the men's side, yes. There was another extension in the ladies' room."

The sheriff laughed. "Bashful, maybe? Did you ask him?"

"Yeah. First he said he didn't think about there being one in there, and then he changed his story and said that he tried the door and it was locked, or stuck. Worked all right when I tried it. And there was nothing inside, either. It was pretty clear that he was lying."

"Joe Searles never had much reputation for telling the truth," Vinge agreed. "So Doc Radebaugh looked at the corpse, did he? That's handy, him being an acting deputy coroner. Where's he now?"

"With the other suspects, in the living room." Sergeant Fischer sensed the sheriff's disapproval and added hastily, "Well, you know Lunney. Before I could stop him he'd told everybody that they were material witnesses and they had to stay until you said they could go. But I handled 'em with kid gloves, Sheriff."

Vinge hesitated, and his thick shoulders sagged. "There's men itching for my job who would change their minds quick enough if they knew what I have to go through," he said, and headed into the house.

Kid gloves or not, their detention had made the people in the Cairns drawing room as jittery as water on a hot stove. They all started talking at once.

"Take it easy, take it easy!" said the sheriff. "We'll have this all straightened out in a few minutes. Don't anybody need to get worried or upset, because all I need from you folks is an informal statement."

"Here's a list of everybody," Officer Lunney whispered, proudly presenting his notebook and then crossing to the front door, where he stood with arms folded.

The sheriff looked at the list, wiped his glasses, and looked again. "Before we start taking the statements," he said almost apologetically, "I'd like to ask Dr. Radebaugh just when the deceased met his death."

Harry Radebaugh, stiff and professional, stood up as if called on to recite in school and said that in his opinion it was not more than two hours ago and not less than one. The post-mortem on the body might cut it down a little closer. But Cairns had come in on the five o'clock and had arrived at the party about twenty minutes after. He'd gone right upstairs and, presumably, almost straight down to his new swimming pool. "Roughly he died between five-thirty and six-fifteen, because it was six-twenty when Miss Abbott came up and found the body on the tiles, covered with a man's blue denim jacket."

"Searles's coat," Sergeant Fischer put in.

The sheriff nodded. "And the phone call from Searles came in at sixteen minutes past six. That all matches right enough."

"If you ask me," Thurlow Abbott suddenly put in, "they should have used a pulmotor on Huntley. Lots of people have been revived after they've been in the water for hours."

Vinge looked towards Dr. Radebaugh, who smiled and said that there could be no question of anything like that in this particular case. "You see, Sheriff, for your information, most deaths in the water come almost immediately, from shock. Cairns was dead when he was hauled out on to the tiles."

"Or else Joe Searles would never have left him there," Sergeant Fischer pointed out. "He'd have shoved him back in."

"Okay," Sheriff Vinge agreed. "Now where was I? Oh, yes. The list. First we have Mr. Thurlow Abbott."

Abbott stood up, and in his ghostly whisper of a voice he insisted that he knew nothing at all about what had happened. Cairns had taken so long to change that he had slipped away from the party and gone up to his son-in-law's room to see what was keeping him, but he had found nobody there and no sign of any disturbance and was on his way downstairs again when he heard the sirens.

"Very good," said the sheriff. "Next, Miss Lawn Abbott."

Lawn leaned against the wall, tapping at her riding shoes with a slender whip. "I'd been out for a ride," she said. "I have a hunter hack that the Boads keep for me in their stable until Huntley—I mean until Huntley could build a stable here. I was later than I realized, because I'm not too good about keeping time, and I didn't get up to the party until just before the police arrived. I saw the body as I came past the pool."

"On your way up the hill did you see anything at all going on at the swimming pool?"

She shook her head. "That's all," said the sheriff. "Next is Mr. and Mrs. Mitchell Beale."

"I was in the library for a while," Midge began with a sidelong glance at Commander Bennington across the room. "Then I danced a little, and after that I played ping-pong. Then everybody started playing bridge, so I wandered into the kitchen. I didn't go outside."

"I didn't leave the living room," Adele put in. "Except once or twice to go up to Helen's room. Once I was looking for her because she was taking so long to change her dress, and once I wanted to fix my hair. I went out on the balcony outside Helen's room to get some air because, to tell the truth, I felt a little swacked."

"When you were out on the balcony did you see any one down at the pool?"

"You can't see the pool from the house because the bathhouse stands right in the way."

Sergeant Fischer was writing away for dear life, trying to take the gist of this down. The sheriff waited for him to catch up and then asked, "Mrs. Beale, I understand there is a stair leading down to the rear patio from the upstairs balcony. You didn't go down that stair, nor see anybody on it?"

Adele shook her head. Sheriff Vinge turned his attention to the Benningtons, obviously anxious to get the whole thing over with as fast as possible. They were quick to inform him that they had been playing bridge in the playroom with Mrs. Boad and Jed Nicolet. Whoever was dummy would go out scouting for drinks or bring in canapes or cigarettes.

"But that would only be for a few minutes at a time, wouldn't it?" The commander agreed that a bridge hand only took around five minutes as a rule, and the sheriff beamed. "We can pass Mrs. Boad and Mr. Nicolet, too, then, because they're accounted for. There's Miss Gertrude Boad—"

Trudy Boad arose, stammering a little, and admitted that for most of the time she had been sitting beside the phonograph, changing records when necessary. She had beaten Mr. Beale four games of ping-pong and later sat in on the bridge game for one hand. "But if you ask my personal opinion about all this—"

"Thank you very much, Miss Boad," said the sheriff firmly, and Trudy's brief moment in the limelight was concluded.

Bill Harcourt, pale and sad with the alcohol dying within him, had the next turn, accounting for his movements sketchily but with some detail. He had never, he admitted, been more than fifty feet from the bar in the dining room. The only contribution he could make was that Cairns had seemed nervous and in a hurry when he arrived home, though that may have been the lateness of the hour and the fact that the man had to rush through a roomful of cocktails without getting one.

That ended that list, to the obvious relief of the sheriff. "We already got statements from the hired help," Sergeant Fischer told him in a whisper. "Name of MacTavish, Jeff and Beulah MacTavish, colored. They been with the Cairnses about four months, and they don't know nothing and they ain't saying nothing, except that they got along fine with Cairns. And here's another list, of the people that were here earlier but left before the body was discovered. They all went away by twos and threes, so I guess we can cross them off."

Sheriff Vinge glanced at the second list, noticed the name of Colonel Wyatt, and was very glad indeed that the colonel had departed earlier enough so that he wouldn't have to be questioned. He did, however, regret not meeting the pair of twins named Leilani and Aloha Linton.

"I guess that's about all," he said to the group. "I suppose, though, I ought to have a word with the widow."

"Naturally my daughter isn't here," Thurlow Abbott said hoarsely. "She's up in her room, completely collapsed."

"Of course, of course. All I was going to ask her was if her husband was in the habit of taking time for a swim before he changed for dinner."

Nobody spoke up to answer that question, although the sheriff looked first at Thurlow Abbott and then at Lawn, who was studiously contemplating the silver knob on her riding crop. Then there came the sound of a thin, strained voice behind them. "How could Huntley have any habits?" cried Helen from the head of the stairs. "Remember, we'd just moved into this house, and the pool was only filled day before yesterday!"

Everybody stared, but Helen was her own mistress again, giving nothing away. She came into the room like a determined sleepwalked and sat down on the edge of a chair. It happened to be the chair in which Dr. Radebaugh was sitting, and he leaned over to touch her arm, but she gave no answering smile.

Officer Lunney came up to the sheriff and whispered for a moment.

Vinge listened and started to shake his head. "But somebody's going to ask that question sometime, Sheriff."

Vinge sighed and turned to Helen. "We weren't going to bother you, Mrs. Cairns. But now that you're here—can you tell us if your husband owned a bathing suit? We were wondering why he went swimming in a sort of corset thingamajig?"

"A—a corset?" she repeated blankly.

"Yes, ma'am. He was wearing it when he was murdered—"

Helen stood up suddenly, her soft mouth drawn into a humorless grin of shock. "Did you say—" Here she tried to catch herself, but her voice spilled over. "You mean it wasn't an accidental drowning? Are you trying to say that Huntley was actually murdered?"

Sheriff Vinge's voice was very gentle. "I'm sorry, ma'am. But that's the way it looks. The story the gardener tells, it won't hold water for a minute. He made it up to cover himself—"

"What does Searles say?" Helen demanded breathlessly.

"Oh, he claims to have seen a strange young man in a blue suit bending over the swimming pool in the very act of killing your husband. According to his story, he locked the killer in the bathhouse—"

Adele Beale took a breath and opened her mouth to speak but shut it again promptly as her husband sank a thumb and forefinger into her left thigh. She glared at Midge, but he was staring off across the room at Helen.

It must be Helen who was making that quick, gasping noise, like a strangled sob. Her eyes were muddy and colorless now, dark-rimmed like holes burned in a blanket. Obviously she had forgotten that they were all staring at her; she was blind to her father's warning glance and to the flash which showed itself ever so briefly in the face of her younger sister.

"Then it *was* Pat!" Helen cried. "He did it—he must have!" She whirled on Midge and Adele, pointing. "You said you saw him on his way here, didn't you?"

The room was so silent that they could have heard a pin drop. And did hear one, as the heavy silver polo-mallet clasp which held Lawn's scarf suddenly came apart in her fingers.

Sheriff Vinge's shoulders slumped a little, as if a great weight had been added. He looked at Helen, took off his glasses to wipe them, and looked again. "I'm afraid, Mrs. Cairns, I'll have to ask you a question. Just who is Pat?"

Helen was biting her lip now, childishly, helplessly. "You'll really have to tell us," Vinge went on. "Now that you've said this much. What's his last name?"

"His name is mud now, thanks to her," Midge Beale whispered. Across the room Helen Cairns suddenly dropped to her knees, burying her face in her arms. She shook her head furiously. She wasn't going to say anything, but it was all too clear that she had said enough already.

Wheels turned, telephones rang, and wires burned. In a very few minutes thin strips of tape began to jerk out of police teletype machines all over Long Island and the metropolitan area of New York, Connecticut, and New Jersey, bearing the message:

NY STATE POLICE GENERAL BROADCAST 75524 FILED 8.25 PM JUNE 16 ALL STATE TROOPERS SHERIFFS CARS LOCAL AUTHORITIES BE ON THE LOOK OUT FOR PAXTON MONTAGUE ALIAS PAT MONTAGUE AGE 25 HEIGHT 5-11 WEIGHT 170 BROWN HAIR HAZEL EYES MILITARY BEARING AND SHORT HAIRCUT WAS LAST SEEN WEARING BLUE SUIT YELLOW NECKTIE BLACK SHOES NO HAT HE MAY BE IN ARMY UNIFORM AS FIRST LIEUTENANT INFANTRY THIS MAN WANTED ON SUSPICION OF HOMICIDE HOLD AND NOTIFY ALBERT VINGE SHERIFF KNIGHT'S COUNTY SHOREHAM LONG ISLAND OR PROVOST MARSHAL CAMP NIVENS NEW YORK END BROADCAST

CHAPTER FOUR

It was a bad night for young men in blue suits and for first lieutenants. All over the metropolitan area of New York, unhappy youths were swept into the police dragnet and charged with being Pat Montague. Those without dog tags, drivers' licenses, or a pocketful of unpaid bills to identify themselves denied it in vain, and half a hundred were locked up on suspicion.

Meanwhile Pat himself perched glumly and alone on a bar stool less than two blocks from the Shoreham police station, wearing no disguise except a dazed expression and a highball glass which he held most of the time before his face. He stared into the murky depths as if the drink were a crystal ball in which his future might be expected to reveal itself. But he saw nothing more than a dingy ice cube, though all the same he had a presentiment of what he was going to be in for.

He went straight up in the air as a heavy hand descended upon his shoulder. His left arm cocked itself, and he was about to let it go when he realized that the police do not go around wearing tropical gabardine suits with a carnation in the buttonhole. The stranger had a pleasant, slightly apologetic smile on his sharp, foxlike face.

"Uk!" gulped Pat Montague.

"Why, I don't mind if I do," Jed Nicolet accepted blandly as he climbed on to the next stool. When the barman had brought him a bottle of ale and a glass, had been paid off and had retired to his hillbilly radio program at the other end of the bar, Jed leaned closer.

"Relax," he advised. "I know who you are from the description. I'm a friend of Helen's."

33

Pat froze. "So?"

"So they tipped me off to look for you around the bars, and there are only three in town. If you don't mind my saying so, it looks as if you need some legal advice." Nicolet produced a business card.

Pat took it. He didn't exactly like this man who looked like a tame, friendly coyote, and yet he had to talk to somebody. "Did Helen send you?"

Nicolet nodded. "Only it was her sister who spoke to me when the police finally let me leave. Helen herself wasn't free to do anything, with the house full of police and the reporters hammering on the door." He took a deep swig of his ale. "You may as well trust me, fellow. What can you lose? Why not break down and tell me just how you fit into all the hell that broke loose up on the hill this afternoon?"

Pat said quickly, "I didn't kill him!" Then he stopped. It wouldn't be any use.

"Start with the moment you got there," Nicolet prompted. "You hadn't been invited, but you knew there was a party. Did Helen know you were in town?"

Pat shook his head. "I called up twice earlier in the week because I wanted to hear her voice. But some maid answered the phone. So I started to walk up there; I can't explain why—"

All the same, he tried explaining through fifteen minutes and two more highballs. Nicolet nodded judicially when it was all finished. "So that's it. It isn't easy to advise you. You could, of course, walk into Sheriff Vinge's office and tell him the story. You could say that you went up to the Cairnses' house uninvited because you wanted just one look at the girl who didn't wait for you while you were overseas. You thought you had a glimpse of her down by the pool, so you climbed down, keeping out of sight of the house. When you got there you happened to look down into the water, and it wasn't Helen, it was Huntley Cairns, and he was dead."

"As a lawyer, give me your opinion."

"As a lawyer, and as a specialist in criminal law and trial cases, I must confess that I don't believe it myself."

Pat flushed and started to slide down off the stool, but the other man caught him by the arm. His muscles, Pat thought, were a lot harder than they looked. "Sit down," Nicolet said firmly. "I don't tell all I know, and this is a privileged communication anyhow. Personally, I think that any one who killed Huntley Cairns ought to be given a gold medal and a key to the city."

"Why?" Pat demanded. "I thought you were a friend of his."

"I put up with him for Helen's sake. But nobody in town liked the man. I've only lived out here a couple of years, but I've seen him racing around burning gasoline in three cars when the rest of us were sweating it out on an A card. He bought a half-interest in the Star Market in town when rationing was tough so he'd have plenty of meat and butter and sugar. And he got a new sedan in February, the only 1946 model in this part of the country. The man made his own rules. Nobody will miss him, not even Helen, if what they say is true."

"Maybe," Pat said slowly. "I wouldn't know about that. But I didn't kill him. Not that I didn't threaten to knock his ears down if we ever met. I already did it once, the night he met Helen. He was on the make then, over three years ago. He didn't have as much dough then, but he was still a louse."

Jed Nicolet nodded. "He had a bad case of Little Man's Disease. He had to keep proving to himself, over and over, that he was better than taller men. Lots of guys have gone to the top through that sort of drive. Anyway, he's dead, and *de mortuis*—"

"I didn't hold him under water until he drowned," Pat insisted. "You've got to accept that or we don't go on talking."

"Okay, you're lily-white. I've had clients who were innocent, now and then. Anyway, I'll see what can be done, for Helen's sake. And because you seem like a nice Joe. Speaking of Helen, you didn't even get to see her, did you?"

"I haven't seen her in three years. Her kid sister gummed up the works— I've always blamed her for it, anyway. I've had a hunch that somebody intercepted my letters and switched telegrams and things. Lawn used to be a little vixen. But she did let me out of that trap today."

Nicolet was calmly sympathetic. "I'm afraid that was no favor. It was bad break number two. If you hadn't run away we'd be in a much sounder position. Never mind that now. What we need is a smoke-screen. Circumstantial evidence is all against you. You had the motive, the means, and the opportunity to kill Huntley Cairns. You are admittedly in love with his wife, and you were on the premises without an invitation. I figure that the police will grab you and tuck you away and mark the case closed, unless—"

"Unless what?"

Jed Nicolet didn't answer for a moment but took a final swig at his glass. "I was just thinking that this is an unusual situation and calls for unusual measures. Suppose it got out to the newspapers and everybody

that you had called in a mastermind private detective, a big-time expert in
murder cases, to get to the bottom of this whole affair."

Pat said glumly that he didn't see it.

"Listen. If we do that, the police won't dare to let the case drop. They'll
realize that they have to keep investigating every possible lead because
they don't want to risk being shown up. The chances are that they'll be
smart enough to call in outside help and eventually turn in the real killer.
And in the meantime we're planting a wedge of doubt that I can hammer
home to the jury when you're on trial."

"On trial for murder," Pat said slowly. "Thanks, but I'm not having
any. All that sort of thing costs big money, too, and I haven't got it."

"Not necessarily. Anyway, it's time somebody else did your thinking.
Come on, I'll drive you down to the hotel. This detective I was telling
you about is staying there in one of the cottages on a hideaway vacation."

Pat suffered himself to be led outside, and they got into an open convertible and went rolling through the village almost down to the shore,
turning in past the Shoreham House, a rambling Victorian firetrap mold-
ering among its bright flower gardens. "The angle to take," Jed Nicolet
warned him, "is strictly Young Love. Whenever you can, strike up 'Hearts
and Flowers,' see?"

"What the hell kind of detective is this?" Pat demanded, but Nicolet
only led him on, around the main building of the hotel and along a little
pebbled walk bordered with clamshells which led to a row of little whitewashed cottages.

"Here we are," Nicolet said cheerfully. He took a deep breath and leaned
on the bell. A moment later a woman faced them; in fact, she looked right
through them as though they didn't exist. She was a lean and angular
person who would never see fifty again and whose face seemed vaguely
to resemble someone Pat had known or seen in the papers. After a moment he realized it was Man o' War.

Jed Nicolet held out his hand. "Well, if it isn't Miss Hildegarde Withers! Glad to find you home. I hope you don't mind our bursting in on you
like this, but I want you to meet my friend Pat Montague, who's just out
of the Army and into a mess of trouble."

She snorted. "And just who are you, young man?" She might have
closed the door, but Jed had his foot in it.

"Nicolet is the name—surely you remember me? We met in court."

The blue-gray eyes spat fire. "We most certainly did! How could I
forget the able counsel for the defense in the bridle-path case! Your client
was found guilty, too, although in the meantime you gave me four hours

of unadulterated torture on the witness stand. And now you have the co-lossal, unmitigated gall to—"

"Come on, Nicolet, let's blow," said Pat dully.

But the young lawyer shook his head. "Miss Withers isn't one to hold a grudge. After all, it was my first case, and I was only trying to do my best for my client." He grinned engagingly. "This is another tough one, ma'am, and I'm hoping to get you on our side. My friend Montague has gone and stuck his head into a noose."

"And you have stuck your foot into my door," the maiden schoolteacher reminded him tartly. "Look, young man! All this won't do you a bit of good. I've retired. I've reformed. I'm through making a nuisance of myself in police matters. Can't you understand that and go away?"

Pat pulled at his sleeve, but the lawyer stood firm. "Miss Withers, I can't believe that you've retired, not with your record of successes."

"My successes, as you call them, were mostly beginner's luck. I was younger and more impetuous in those days. As Emerson, a very fine poet you have no doubt never read, once said, 'It is time to be old, to take in sail.' "

Jed Nicolet smiled. "That's from *Terminus*. I'll give you a topper—the same poet wrote something about life never being so short but that there is time for courtesy. And he said, ' 'Tis man's perdition to be safe, when for the truth he ought to die!' "

The spinster seemed to soften just a little, and then she shook her head again. "I've still retired. There's an excellent precedent. Even Sherlock Holmes retired, you know. He went off to keep bees in the country. Well, I've taken a leaf out of his book, only not to keep bees because I hate the nasty, stinging things."

"You chose tropical fish instead!" interrupted Nicolet, looking past the schoolteacher towards the big glass tank in the front window. "I got into that once. Lots of fun. But is it exciting enough for a person like yourself, with your capacity for mystery and adventure?"

She hardened her heart. "Besides, gentlemen, I have problems of my own at the moment. I have a *scalare*, an angelfish, which is in worse trouble than you are. If you'll excuse me—"

Jed Nicolet winked at Pat and turned back to the schoolma'am. "That is a shame," he said. "I suppose you found him leaning sideways, and then after a while he floated up to the top of the tank?"

Miss Withers stared at him blankly, and then her face cracked into something of a smile. "So you do know fish! Yes, it was like that. Yet I did everything they said. It's a twenty-gallon tank, with indirect lighting and water that was ripened for two whole weeks, and there's an aerator and two heaters and umpteen varieties of aquarium plants. I've kept the temperature at seventy-seven degrees, I've—"

"Salt water is the only thing," Nicolet advised her. "Put the fish into a panful of warm water with half a cup of salt. I'll show you, if I may."

Miss Withers hesitated and was lost. A moment later Nicolet was fishing the dying *scalare* from the marine wonderland, the miniature world of bright yellow sand and softly plumed Paris-green plants, through which a score or so of tiny jeweled fishes floated, like Disney drawings come to life.

"Swinburne," Jed Nicolet said, "wasn't kidding when he wrote so much about our mother the sea. The blood in our veins is almost identical with sea water, less the corpuscles, of course. It's that way with fish too. Dying salmon carried out to sea at the mouth of a river usually survive." He dumped the limp angelfish into the saline solution, where it floated helplessly at the surface. Not even its gill fins were moving, and the broad bands of velvety black which normally striped its body were faded to a dull brownish-gray.

Pat Montague, all this while, stood by the door, waiting for a chance to make an exit. But nobody was paying him the slightest attention. He could, he reflected, go to the chair for all they cared.

The lawyer and Miss Withers bent over the lifeless fish. "Too late, I'm afraid," she was saying. "It's the end of poor Gabriel."

"And it looks like the end of me!" Pat put in. "If you—"

"Hush!" said Jed Nicolet. He was gently swishing the water around in the saucepan. Suddenly he gave a sharp exclamation as there came a faint flicker of the transparent gill fins, a movement of the goggled mouth. And then the angelfish Gabriel miraculously wriggled, fought drunkenly back to an even keel.

"So what does it all prove?" Pat demanded. "I suppose if we'd put the body of Huntley Cairns into warm salt water he'd have—"

Jed Nicolet waved at him to shut up.

"I do believe he's coming round," Miss Withers admitted. "I'm grateful to you, Mr. Nicolet, although of course I understand perfectly why you did it. All the same, I'll have to listen to your friend's story."

Suddenly given the floor, Pat couldn't think of anything to say. How was he going to tell his tale to this acidulous old maid? How could he explain to her about Helen and everything?

"The last time I saw her," he said, "we had been out dancing somewhere, and she wore a white dress or maybe it was a suit. It was daylight when I brought her home, and she came out on the little balcony outside her father's apartment to wave down at me. Somehow she's still waving at me—time stopped still that night—and she'll go on waving until I see her again. But I guess you wouldn't understand."

"Don't be so sure," the schoolteacher snapped. "Believe it or not, but I've had my chances. Go on."

"It seemed like fate," Pat said. "I read in the paper that Helen was living out here in Shoreham and that she was giving a housewarming. I thought maybe I'd crash the party. At least I could see her and find out if she was happy and hear it from her own lips if it had to be good-bye." He talked on and on and finally stopped.

Miss Withers sighed. "It is one of the saddest things in this life," she said, "that two people rarely fall out of love at the same time."

Pat insisted doggedly that he didn't believe Helen had ever fallen out of love with him. Her father and especially her sister had been after her to marry Cairns, that fat, hairy little kewpie of a man. He'd been away in camp, and something went wrong with the letters and telegrams he sent, but that must have been Lawn Abbott's work.

"The Wicked Sister, eh?" Miss Withers smiled faintly. "All the rest of it seems like an unfortunate coincidence, with the gardener leaping to an erroneous but very natural conclusion. I don't see that you have very much to worry about. Contrary to public opinion, the police do not want to pin crimes on innocent bystanders." Then suddenly she was silent. "Just a minute, young man. Did I understand you to say that Huntley Cairns was *fat*?"

Both Pat and Nicolet admitted that Cairns was a tub of a man, not over five feet six and weighing around two hundred pounds. Miss Withers nodded. "And when you saw the body it was at the bottom of the deep end of the swimming pool?"

Pat Montague nodded.

"Excuse me just a minute," said the schoolteacher. "I must make a telephone call." She went into the bedroom, closing the door behind her, and then for a few moments busied herself by fluttering the pages of a number of extremely thick and solid volumes. She found what she wanted, nodded slowly, and then picked up the phone.

In the living room Jed Nicolet was reassuring his client. "It's going over big. She's on our side, and the police won't be so quick to try to hang a murder rap on you—"

Then the door opened and Miss Withers appeared. "Before we go any further, gentleman, there is something you ought to know."

The two young men looked up at her wonderingly.

"It's only this," the schoolteacher announced. "I just called up the Shoreham police and reported your presence here."

CHAPTER FIVE

Jerked to their feet, both Montague and Jed Nicolet goggled at her. "Oh, you're quite free to escape," Miss Withers advised them. "If the police arrive and find you gone they will understand that one poor weak woman couldn't hold anybody by force. But honestly, I don't think you'd get very far if you made a run for it, Mr. Montague. The police may have their limitations, but they are very efficient about such things as dragnets and manhunts."

There was no compassion in her. "It serves you right, of course," she told Pat Montague, "for trying to take me in with a cock-and-bull story like that."

"What's wrong with the story?" Nicolet found his voice first, and his tone indicated to Miss Withers that he was willing and anxious to have his client change or amend his testimony in any possible way if only she would tell him how.

"The flaw is something that cannot be repaired," she continued almost chattily. "You see, I happen to have read that a fat man has considerably less specific gravity than a thin man—and even a thin man will usually float well above the bottom of any body of water when first drowned. So you see? Huntley Cairns couldn't have been dead at the bottom of his own swimming pool, not unless you were holding him down. He would probably have been floating almost halfway to the surface, as a matter of fact."

"But wait a minute," Nicolet began to argue. "The man had drowned, and his lungs were full of water—"

"Not necessarily. In many cases of drowning—of which, according to your account of the doctor's preliminary investigation, this is one—death comes by asphyxia almost immediately, and little or no water enters the respiratory tract. Look it up for yourself in Webster, or Sydney Smith, or Glaister, or Witthaus and Becker. Smith also points out that in the case of a newborn child, where there is an excess of fat, the body will usually refuse to sink at all!"

Pat Montague, dazed but dogged, shook his head. "I don't care what it says in the books, I've told you the truth. He was at the bottom of the deep end of the pool. His eyes were wide open and staring, and the water rippled a little, so that he seemed to be making faces and grinning at me."

"It all sounds very convincing," Miss Withers snapped. "But you stick to your story and I'll stick with Sydney Smith."

"If my client wanted to lie," Nicolet objected, "I'm sure he could make up a better lie than that. After all—"

"Just how and when did I get to be your client, anyhow?" Pat Montague finally exploded. "I don't remember asking you to come barging into this mess. I was doing all right by myself. I could have been halfway to the Canadian border by now. But, oh, no, you had to drag me here so I could meet this wonderful mastermind amateur sleuth who right away runs and screams for the police!"

"Take it easy," Nicolet snapped. "Wait a minute—"

"A minute is about all the free time I've got. Personally, I think you've been bucking for a pop in the face, and—"

"Gentlemen, please!" cried Miss Hildegarde Withers nervously. Then there came a heavy knock at the door, and both the embattled warriors froze in position, fists cocked, as if they were acting out some old Currier and Ives print.

The schoolteacher hastily flung the door open, to look into the faces of two young patrolmen from the radio car. "You're just in time to referee!" she greeted them.

"Evening, ma'am. Thanks for calling us. All right, Montague, you're coming with us."

"Just one minute," interposed the schoolteacher.

The officer stiffened. "Now it won't do any good to change your mind and ask us to let him go, because the sheriff give us strict orders."

"It's only this," she explained gently. "You're arresting the wrong man. That is Mr. Nicolet. This is Mr. Montague here."

"My mistake," the officer cheerily admitted. "Come to think of it, this one does fit the description a little better. Sorry, Mr. Nicolet. Come on, you. Let's get going."

So it was that Pat Montague went out of the cottage handcuffed to the thick wrist of a policeman who was whistling "It Might as Well Be Spring" considerably off key. The other officer followed after thanking Miss Withers again.

Jed Nicolet lingered for a moment in the doorway. "I've only one thing to say, Miss Withers. Maybe I was a little rough on you in court, but, lady, we're even now!" Then he went out, almost but not quite slamming the door.

"And that," said Miss Hildegarde Withers to herself, "is that." She had nobly resisted temptation and kept her promise to the inspector. "I ought to get a gold star, or at least an E for effort," she added.

There was nothing whatever to worry about. And she still had her tropical fish. She turned back gratefully to the aquarium, where everything was serene. She had found it very soothing of late to lose herself in that lambent green fairyland, to sit for hours staring into the water world, until she felt as if she herself belonged there. "I must be a mermaid at heart," she decided.

The neon tetras were glowing with their eerie brilliance; the head-and-tail lights had their signals all turned on, fore and aft. The blue moons were shining; the hatchet fish skipped about on the surface, threatening to take off at any moment, and the common ordinary run-of-the-mill guppies and mollies circulated in the background like extra people on a moving picture set.

Even the dojos and catfish and snails, at the very bottom of this social structure, went about their scavenging peacefully, stirring up muddy sand with their busy noses. It was a peace not entirely shared by Miss Withers, whose conscience was of the New England variety. Even though, as she kept assuring herself, she had done what was obviously the right and proper thing.

However, she jerked to the alert like an old fire horse as the doorbell sounded. It turned out to be Jed Nicolet again, his sharp face smiling quizzically through the crack in the open door.

"Sorry, ma'am," he said. "I know how you feel, and all that. I don't exactly blame you. But, anyway, I had to come back to tell you. Don't forget to take that sick *scalare* out of the salt water or he'll fold up again. Half an hour is plenty."

Surprised, Miss Withers turned back to the saucepan, where Gabriel was now swimming easily, his color restored. Nicolet watched as she dumped the tiny fish back into the tank, where it at once took up its place beside its cruising mate.

"Good as new, isn't he?" Nicolet observed. "Remember that trick if you have any more trouble, which you probably won't, because most of your fish are hardy types." Then he scowled suddenly as a magnificently iridescent fish swam out of the plant forest, trailing long blue-green plumes like some sort of marine peacock. Behind him, at a respectful distance, tagged a paler, more streamlined female. "Oh-oh! Lady, you may have trouble with those *bettas* in a community tank. That female—"

"Nonsense!" Miss Withers shook her head firmly. "She's the best-behaved fish in the aquarium. As a matter of fact, nobody but the angelfish ever chase the smaller fry."

"Female *bettas* have a bad name," Jed Nicolet insisted. "I never had any trouble with them, but—"

"Now, look here, young man," the schoolteacher challenged. "You didn't come back here to talk about fish. There's something else on your mind. I suppose you think it was reasonable of me to call the police, don't you? It was my obvious duty as a citizen, you know."

"I suppose so," he agreed absently. "Otherwise you would have been technically an accessory after the fact, or at least guilty of harboring a fugitive from justice." He looked up at her suddenly. "You really think that Montague is guilty, then?"

"Why else would he tell such a whopping big lie?"

Nicolet shrugged his shoulders. "I only met the fellow tonight, so I can't say. He didn't seem the type—"

"The type to murder, or the type to lie? In my opinion, he is just a smart young man who realizes that if you look a person straight in the eye and have a firm handclasp you'll get by with any story." Miss Withers firmly replaced the cover on the fish tank. "And now I'm going to ask you something. Why have you taken such a great interest in helping him?"

"Why, I was asked to." Nicolet was looking at the wall, where there was nothing of interest except a framed portrait of the graduating class of 1916 at Teachers College.

"You were asked by Mrs. Cairns or her sister?"

He nodded. "But that isn't quite all. I was pretty sure that somebody else killed Huntley Cairns."

"Who?" demanded the schoolteacher. "Not that it makes the slightest difference to me, you understand."

Nicolet hesitated, his face puzzled and thoughtful. There was a trace of some other emotion, perhaps it was relief. "Oh, nobody in particular," he finally sidestepped. "It's just that there didn't seem motive enough for Pat to kill Cairns. I wouldn't kill a man just because I was in love with his wife."

"Then just what," queried Miss Withers grimly, "would you kill for?"

If she had expected that to set him back on his heels she was sadly disappointed. "People kill," he said, "to pay somebody back when things can't be evened up any other way. Or to save their necks. Or for gain— *cui bono*, as we say."

" 'For whose advantage.' " The schoolteacher nodded.

"That's it. You saw Pat Montague. Could you honestly believe that he'd murder a man in a particularly cold-blooded manner five minutes after he'd met him?"

"I can believe anything," Miss Withers said firmly. "Why, sometimes I've believed as many as six impossible things before breakfast, like the White Queen."

"Then all I can say is, I hope you're not on the jury," Jed Nicolet told her. "I guess I've been talking too much. Sorry I tried to drag you into this thing, but it seemed to be right up your alley." The door closed behind him, very softly this time.

Feeling strangely nettled for a lady who has just had her own way, scored a success and proved a point, Miss Hildegarde Withers went mechanically around the room emptying ashtrays and turning out lights. She paused before turning out the long fluorescent tube over the aquarium, watching for a moment the graceful parading of the angelfish, the florid strutting of the male *betta* back and forth before the little mirror she had fastened outside the tank to make him think he had a rival.

"Men!" said Miss Withers. Behind the *Betta splendens* swam the worshipping female, her eyes filled with pride and admiration, seeing nothing in all the universe except her mate. All was serene in that little world. The fat black mollies nibbled at the fronds of the trailing plants like grazing sheep, the guppies circled and scattered and gathered again like sparrows in a barnyard, and the neon tetras—

No, there was but one neon on display. The other had no doubt gone to bed somewhere in the shadows of the plant jungle. "Setting me an excellent example," declared Miss Withers, and snapped the switch. Instantly the fairyland became only a big glass box full of water and weeds, and the jeweled fish were dull minnows.

The schoolteacher brushed her hair the usual one hundred times and then sought her couch, but something—perhaps pride in her mild tri-

umph of the evening—kept her tossing. She finally gave in and took a
bromide, sinking after a while into a semi-slumber in which one nightmare followed another, overlapping like a montage.

She was under the surface of the water in all of them, swimming fran-
tically, with something vague and implacable following wherever she
went.

Then she woke up suddenly to hear her doorbell buzzing its angry,
intermittent summons. According to the little red leather traveling clock
which the inspector had given her once for Christmas—quite possibly as
a hint she was getting into his hair—it was not quite ten in the morning.
She climbed wearily into bathrobe and slippers. If this was that young
lawyer again, she would send him off with his ears burning.

But it was a girl who stood in the doorway, a girl in a white blouse over
riotous tropical slacks. Her face was pale and striking, almost stark in
fact, without color except for the lips. "Her mother must have been fright-
ened by a Martha Graham dance group," the schoolteacher decided.

"I'm Lawn Abbott," the girl announced in a low, husky contralto. "I
must see you."

Miss Withers suddenly became very wide awake indeed. "You may
come in, child," she said. "But I tell you in advance that I won't be able to
help you."

The girl came into the room, sat down on the edge of the chair Miss
Withers had indicated, and then immediately rose and started pacing up
and down. She was acting rather like a cat in a strange place. There was
something else of the cat about her too—a rather attractive something.
She was no silky Persian, no alley cat on the defensive, but rather a Siamese
or Burmese, thin and feminine and strong.

Finally she spoke. "I didn't come here to ask for your help. I came here
to help you—to set you straight about something. You see, Jed Nicolet
called up last night and told me all about being here and everything. Helen
is completely prostrated, of course, and Father is no use at a time like
this. I tried to see Pat, but they wouldn't let me. They wouldn't even let
me talk to him on the phone. I suppose you know that Sheriff Vinge booked
him for murder because of what you told the police. Miss Withers, have
you seen the Sunday morning papers?"

"Naturally not, my dear. You awakened me."

"Well, it's time that somebody woke you up!" Lawn's voice did not
rise, but there was a thin, metallic ring to it now. "Because you don't
know that there was a ragged tear in the shorts that Huntley was wearing
when he died! The police at first thought it must have been made by the

rake which, according to their theory, held him under when he was drowning—"

"I'm really not very interested."

"But you've got to be interested! Pat is innocent as a newborn babe; anybody with half an eye could see that. I knew it when I found him in that bathhouse. If I can prove it to you will you help me convince the police so they'll let him go?"

Miss Withers sniffed. "Unless my memory is failing, Pat Montague was supposed to have been an old beau of your sister's. Just why are you entering the picture?"

"Because …" Lawn bit her lip. "Never mind why. I'm mixed up in it too. The police were very nasty about my unlocking that door until good old Jed pointed out that I couldn't have known who was inside. Naturally I want to prove Pat innocent. Will you help?"

"I'm afraid it would take a good deal to convince the police that Pat Montague isn't their man."

"Oh, nonsense and stuff! Only last night that fool of a sheriff was positive that he had it all pinned on poor old Searles. Tomorrow it may be somebody else—Jed, or father, or me. I just want Pat out of jail, that's all."

"There would have to be some new evidence," Miss Withers said.

"How about this?" Lawn dramatically held up her right hand, showing that the fleshy part of the index finger had been covered with adhesive tape. Underneath was a deep, ragged cut. "They're draining the pool this morning," the girl continued. "But I didn't wait for that. I sneaked out and went for a swim before daylight, and I dived down into the corner where they found Huntley's body. I felt around down there until I caught my finger on a jagged bit of metal—part of the circular cap that goes around the outlet. It must have been damaged in putting it in. Anyway, what I'm trying to point out is this. If Huntley's shorts were caught on that hook, wouldn't his body have stayed at the bottom until somebody pulled it loose?"

Miss Withers didn't say anything.

"It's your move," Lawn challenged. "You got Pat where he is. You can get him out."

"Come and sit down while I make a cup of coffee," the schoolteacher conceded. "I'm afraid that it is possible, as you indicate, that I drew my conclusions on insufficient evidence." She started to measure the coffee into the pot. "But I think what you really want isn't just to get Pat Montague out of jail. You want him completely cleared, and that can't happen until we find the real murderer. Are you sure that will make you happy?"

Lawn hesitated.

"These family affairs can be very difficult. You and your father have lived with your sister Helen ever since she married Cairns, haven't you? Forgive my frankness, but he must have been very much in love with Helen to take on her whole family too."

"Or impressed with father. Father used to be famous, you know. He was on Broadway in *The Red Mill* and *Graustark* and *The Chocolate Soldier*, things like that."

"And was Helen very much in love with her husband?"

"You'd better ask her that."

"I would, but she wouldn't answer. Look, child, I'm only trying to get the background. I'm not just prying."

"Well, then," Lawn admitted, "I'd say that Helen isn't emotionally mature enough to love anybody except herself. The love affair between Helen and Helen should go down in history, like *Romeo and Juliet*. Oh, I'll admit that she had a sort of crush on Pat long ago, just boy-and-girl stuff, but she was a good wife to Huntley. Helen was cut out to be a rich man's wife, designed perfectly for the life he could give her. They fitted like—like a picture and a frame."

"You wanted your sister to marry Cairns, didn't you? Was it because he had money?"

Lawn looked puzzled. "I certainly wasn't opposed to it, not knowing Helen as I did, and do."

"According to what I have heard, you did your best to break up Pat's romance with your sister so that she would fall into Huntley Cairns's waiting arms."

The girl's pale, mask-like face showed no expression. "Did Pat say that?"

Miss Withers didn't answer. "It must have been Pat," Lawn decided. "Jed Nicolet wouldn't have—he's a good friend of mine."

"It is true, isn't it?"

Lawn suddenly put down the cup of coffee, which she had barely tasted. "Truth!" she exploded. Then she rose and turned towards the other room. She was not walking catlike now, but heavily and dully, as if all the starch and spring had gone out of her. "Please forget that I came here," she said. "Just forget the whole thing." And she went out, leaving the door open.

"Well!" murmured Miss Hildegarde Withers. She closed the door, bringing back with her the New York morning papers. She could not resist turning to the somewhat meager stories about the Shoreham murder while she sipped her coffee. It would certainly do no harm to see what the papers said, especially since the choice had been made so easy for her. She wasn't going to get mixed up in the case; everybody, including herself, seemed determined about that.

There was a photograph of Huntley Cairns, evidently taken some years ago when he had been on a Defense Bond committee. He looked placid and pleased with himself. There was also a picture of what this particular paper at least had decided upon as the murder weapon, a garden rake held firmly in the hand of Officer Ray Lunney, in a somewhat smeary flash-light photo taken beside the Cairns swimming pool. There was another photograph of the strange, torn garment which the dead man had been wearing.

That was all the press had been able to uncover, or else the Sunday edition had been put to bed too early for any more of the gory details.

Miss Withers pushed aside the newspapers without even reading the comics. Not even Dick Tracy or Barnaby's fairy godfather could inspire her now. But she had given up detecting, she reminded herself, and by a determined effort set her mind back upon the proper track Crossing the room, she turned on the light over the aquarium. Gabriel, the angelfish, was fine and well this morning. She dumped some powdered food into the feeding triangle, watched it cascade down as the fish wildly gobbled at it. There was still only one neon tetra in evidence, and try as she might, Miss Withers could nowhere catch a glimpse of the flash of glowing, living light which should have been in its mate. Perhaps it was sulking.

Then with a start of horror she caught sight of a spot of grisly activity in the rear of the tank behind the red rock. A midget skeleton moved erratically on the sand, whirling end over end.

Two busy Japanese snails and a spotted eel-like king dojo were fulfilling their ghoulish task of cleaning up the tank. The dead fish was disposed of, all except skull and spine. As Miss Withers turned away, feeling faintly ill, the doorbell summoned her once more.

"Botheration!" muttered the schoolteacher. She thought that she might just let it go on ringing. But curiosity was her besetting sin, and she could no more have refrained from seeing who this visitor was than she could have stopped breathing.

This time a womanish girl in black stood in the doorway, a full-bosomed girl with soft brown hair and deep aquamarine eyes, soot-bordered now from sleeplessness. Behind her, fidgeting slightly and out of breath, was a much older man. He reminded Miss Withers of the "men of distinction" in the whiskey advertisements, and smelled as she imagined they would smell.

"Are you Miss Hildegarde Withers?" Thurlow Abbott began, his voice a harsh, croaking whisper.

"That is I," answered the schoolteacher.

"We owe you an apology for breaking in on you like this—"

"Oh, stop it, Father!" The girl in black was coldly angry. "We want to know what my sister has been saying to you! What lies has she been telling now? Don't try to deny it; we know that Lawn was just here." She subsided, on the verge of hysteria.

"You must be Helen Cairns," Miss Withers said. "Please come in and sit down."

Helen shook her head. "My father and I can't stop. We have to get back. But we want to know what Lawn said to you."

"I'm very sorry, Mrs. Cairns, but—"

"As if we didn't know already!" Helen exploded. "She wanted to make my husband's death look like murder, didn't she? She's got the idea that you have some sort of connection with the police, and she's trying to frame poor Pat, who never hurt any one in his whole life! Can't you see?"

"You don't know me, Mrs. Cairns," Miss Withers said, with a sniff, "but I am not a person easily used. Tell me, why should your sister Lawn try to do all these things?"

Father and daughter exchanged a long look. "My daughter Lawn's motives have always been a complete mystery to me," Thurlow Abbott said hoarsely. "This will sound strange to you, coming from a father, but sometimes I have thought that, just as some girls have a vocation for the Church, Lawn has a vocation for *evil*!"

The schoolteacher's eyebrows went up. Then she turned back to Helen. "Mrs. Cairns, did you know that Pat Montague telephoned you twice last week from the separation center at Camp Nivens?"

Helen shook her head slowly. "I didn't know until last night that Pat was within two thousand miles of here. Lawn must have answered the phone, because Beulah would have taken a message or at least told me that someone called."

"But couldn't Mr. Montague have told the difference between the maid's voice and your sister's?"

Helen shook her head wearily. "Not if Lawn answered the phone in a stage colored accent, the way she does sometimes, with a 'Mistah Cyains's res'dence.' "

"Lawn has a most peculiar sense of humor at times," Thurlow Abbott explained.

Miss Withers frowned. "Suppose we leave, just for a moment, the subject of the Wicked Sister," she said. "Just who, Mrs. Cairns, do you think killed your husband—if it wasn't Pat Montague?"

There was nothing but silence in answer to that shot, so the school-teacher went blithely on: "You're not, of course, trying to suggest that Lawn herself might have done it?"

Helen Cairns suddenly broke into laughter, thin, clear, mirthless laughter. "*Lawn?* Lawn murder Huntley? Don't be ridiculous. She never liked him much, though she enjoyed the allowance he gave her and the nice soft life she had with us. But do you imagine for a minute that she would kill him—and leave *me* free, with Pat coming back?"

"You see," Abbott put in, "my daughter has a theory that Lawn has been secretly in love with Pat Montague since she was sixteen."

"She used to tag around after Pat and me like a—like a shadow," Helen went on. "She had a schoolgirl crush on Pat, and she clung for years to a silly toy monkey that he'd bought her when we were all at a night club. She's been waiting like a harpy to pounce on him when he got back out of the Army, because she thought that with me married and out of the way she'd have clear sailing."

Miss Withers thought that over. "Well, eliminating Mr. Montague, and your sister, and the gardener, and everybody else—then who did kill Huntley Cairns? Am I correct in supposing that you are here to ask me to try to find out?"

"Why, yes," Thurlow Abbott began. "In a way I mean—because they say you have had experience in such affairs—"

"But on second thought," Helen said very firmly, with a look at her father, "it might be better after all to let the regular police handle it. Now that you understand about my sister and all—"

"I don't understand," Miss Withers said shortly. "With one breath you accuse her of trying to frame Pat Montague, and with the next you say that she is in love with him."

Helen was silent, confused.

"Perhaps my daughter was simply suggesting that 'Hell hath no fury like a woman scorned,' " Abbott pronounced. "Lawn is a very strange girl."

"I said more than I meant to say," Helen chimed in suddenly. "Besides, there can't be much doubt but that Huntley was swimming in the pool and got caught on a bit of metal so that he drowned accidentally." She turned to go.

"Can't there, though!" murmured Miss Withers as she leaned from her front window and watched them drive away in a long, sleek sedan. "This is murder, if I ever saw it. I'm very much afraid that in spite of all my good resolutions and my promises I am going to have to exercise a woman's privilege and change my mind." But first there was something to get straight. She put in a long-distance call to Inspector Oscar Piper at his home but found that he was not in. He had been called down to Centre Street a little while ago. Mrs. McFeeters, his fumbling elderly housekeeper, wanted to know if there was any message.

Miss Withers thought not. This would be easier to handle in person, anyway, and after the peace and quiet of the country she had a sudden nostalgic longing for the smells of Manhattan, the hum of its activity. Besides, there were a number of errands she could do in town, even though it was a Sunday.

Downtown in the grim environs of Centre Street, Inspector Oscar Piper sat at his battered oak desk in the inner office of the homicide bureau, deep in official papers. Only a skeleton staff was on duty, so Miss Withers was able to barge in upon him with a minimum of delay. He immediately put aside an extremely grisly photograph of some deceased citizen reclining upon a marble slab and laid aside the gnawed butt of his cigar.

"Go right ahead and smoke," she said. "I don't mind."

The grizzled little Irishman stared at her. "What's come over you?" he demanded. "Must be that the simple life agrees with you. How's the goldfish?"

Miss Withers looked upon her old friend and sparring partner with a sudden flash of her gray-blue eyes. "They are not goldfish!"

"Okay, tropical fish, then. As long as they keep you out of my hair—"

"I could ask, 'What hair?' but I won't. Because, Oscar, I want you to relieve me of a promise I made you some time ago."

"Oh-oh! You're weakening already, huh?"

"It's not quite like that. I want to meddle in this particular case because so many people have made it clear that they don't want me to. And especially because a young man appealed to me for help last night and I let him down. But don't look so long-faced, Oscar. It's that swimming-pool murder out at Shoreham, so it won't be in your territory and I won't be in your way."

The wiry little Irishman stood up suddenly, turning to address a large photograph of ex-Mayor La Guardia which somebody had forgotten to remove from the wall. "She says she won't be getting in my way!" he cried. "This I have got to see!"

"Now, Oscar!"

"Don't you now-Oscar me! For your information, I just got word from the commissioner. Sheriff Vinge, out at Shoreham, feels that he is getting a little over his depth and has requested help from the department. Guess who is the lucky boy?"

"Oh, dear!" murmured Miss Hildegarde Withers. Then an elfish smile illuminated her long, horsy face. "Hold on to your hat, Oscar. Here we go again!"

CHAPTER SIX

"When I make a mistake," remarked Miss Hildegarde Withers to the blurred panorama of Long Island's ash dumps which flitted past her train window, "I make a beaut!"

A mile or so farther along the way she added: "But after all, it's the murderer who can't afford to make a mistake. He has only to be wrong once for us to succeed—we have only to be right once."

And as she left the train at Shoreham Station and waited for a taxicab she concluded: "However, I've certainly proved to myself once more that a little information, like a little learning, is a dangerous thing. I must find out what really happened at that cocktail party."

But where, exactly, to begin? The schoolteacher knew that a direct frontal attack, today at least, was out of the question. The Cairns house would be by now completely taken over by the police. The inspector, together with the car and driver supplied him by the department, would be there by now, and he was not in a mood to put up with her being underfoot.

Besides, he knew his business. The machine was unimaginative but thorough. There would be no clues passed over, no statements unchecked. It would be her problem to milk the inspector dry of whatever information he dug up, but that could come later. In the meantime …

"Go roundabout!" had been Peer Gynt's counsel from the Boyg. Miss Withers was not at all sure what a Boyg was, but the advice seemed sound. She would sneak up on this murder from the side. At this point in her reveries one of the town's two taxicabs arrived, emblazoned with the "Busted Duck" insignia of the honorably discharged veteran, and she told the driver approximately where she wanted to go.

He brightened on learning that it was to be a rather longer haul than usual. At the end of the ride he leaned back to open the door, indicating the second house from the corner. "That's it," he advised her. "One of Mame Boad's old firetraps. Richest woman in this town. I used to work for her before I got drafted—she keeps her dog kennels in fine shape, but her tenants can make their own repairs."

Miss Withers agreed that there should be a special level of hell's hottest corner reserved for the nation's landlords and asked the young man to wait. As she went up the walk she noticed that the lawn needed cutting and saw that there was a small convertible parked in the driveway with one front wheel in a bed of nasturtiums.

Upstairs in the front bedroom Adele Beale lay snoring, with her face buried deep in a down pillow. A familiar, insistent voice tugged her back to life.

"Wake up, will you? Wa-a-a-ake up!"

The pillow was forcibly removed, and Midge Beale stared down critically at the wife of his bosom, who had retired last night without removing her war paint or doing up her hair and who now looked like something special in the way of hags. "Go away and let me die in peace," she moaned. "I can't stand the thought of breakfast."

"Never mind breakfast, I didn't make any. But wake up!"

She opened one eye. "Midge! It isn't even light yet!"

"It's getting dusk, you mean. Come on."

"Midge, listen. I had the damnedest nightmare—"

Midge Beale had long since lost interest in Adele's dreams, though she loved to tell them in detail. "Anyway," he cut in, "it was no nightmare about Huntley Cairns. It happened, all right. Snap out of it. Remember, they kept us up there until all hours, and when we finally got home we killed a bottle?" He shook her shoulder. "Come on downstairs, we got company."

Adele sat up suddenly, pushing the hair back from her eyes. "Reporters?"

He shook his head. "No reporters, so stop primping. It's a funny old battleaxe in a hat that looks like a fruit salad. She's trying to dig up some evidence to get Pat Montague out of jail. She says she's an old aunt of his or something."

"Tie a can to her! Tell her—"

"I tried to, and I couldn't make it stick."

"I don't think I can stand up," Adele complained. "And I must look like a perfect fright."

Midge nodded. "How much would you charge to haunt a house?"

"How many rooms?" Adele countered, unsmiling. She ran a comb through her hair, stuck on another mouth over the old one, and slipped into a shapeless pink garment trimmed with maribou. Then, clinging to the banister, she made her way slowly down the stairs. She stopped half-way. "Now don't tell her *anything*!" she whispered fiercely.

"Perish the thought," Midge agreed.

In the living room Miss Hildegarde Withers was sitting on one of the wicker chairs, her feet firmly planted on a Navajo rug. "Forgive me, Mrs. Beale, for getting you up at this hour," she began. "But when murder strikes in a little town like this we are all involved until it's settled."

"If murder did have to strike, it was just as well it landed on Huntley Cairns, who is so easily spared," Midge said.

"That's your opinion!" Adele snapped. "If you knew as much as you think you know …" She caught herself. "Anyway, in my opinion, it was only an accident anyhow, and I'm sure that Midge and I know nothing about it. I don't see why you came to us, anyway—"

"That, my dear, was because you two are almost the only ones on the list of sus—the list of material witnesses that I had not had the pleasure of meeting previously."

"You're wasting your time, I'm afraid," Adele said wearily.

"Perhaps I am. I have plenty to waste. I'm quite sure that neither of you had anything to do with the murder. But could we please start at the beginning? Did you have any business dealings with Mr. Cairns?"

The schoolteacher was speaking to Midge Beale, but Adele answered quickly, her eyes flashing. "No, of course not! Why should I—I mean we?"

"I'm just a test pilot," Midge went on. "Right now I'm flying a T-square, though. I only knew Cairns to speak to, but Adele—"

"I knew him slightly years ago. But Helen is one of my nearest and dearest friends."

The schoolteacher nodded. "I see. Does either of you, by the way, think that Pat Montague could have murdered Cairns?"

"Nope!" Midge said quickly.

"Yes!" cried his wife. "Because if he didn't, then who did? Oh, I guess that isn't a very nice thing to say to one of his relatives, but it's what I think."

Miss Withers hesitated. "I'm afraid I should admit to you that I am an aunt to Pat Montague only pro tem and by adoption. But I had to get in to talk to you somehow. Never mind that, Mrs. Beale. You say that you think Pat did it, and a moment ago you said you thought Cairns died by accident."

"I only meant—"

"Never mind. If it was murder, Pat Montague may be guilty, but not for the reasons I thought last night. That is why, since I was responsible for his being dragged away to jail, I am now trying to get him out. Or at least sworn to get to the bottom of this mystery." She beamed at them. "Come now, can't either of you suggest a reason why somebody would want to kill Huntley Cairns?"

Adele shook her head. "It's early in the evening for me to play guessing games."

"I know from nothing," Midge said. "I wouldn't even have gone to that party if I hadn't been dragged by the scruff of the neck."

"Well, you enjoyed it after you got there, I noticed! I saw you dancing with Helen, and if you'd had a sandwich in your pocket it would have been on toast in two minutes!"

Midge blinked. "Okay! I'll bet your only reason for insisting that we go to the party was so that you could see Huntley Cairns again! Why don't you tell the lady why you once crowned him with a plate, darling? That was before we were married, when you were going around with him. Weren't you even making a pitch to marry him?"

Miss Withers sank deeper and deeper into her chair, trying to look as if she weren't there. The Beales' hangovers made them seem inclined to play truth and consequences.

"That was years and years ago! If you think I'm still carrying a torch for Huntley …" Adele whirled on the schoolteacher. "Just so you won't get any wrong ideas from my loudmouthed husband, it all happened one night when we were out at the Sands Point Country Club. Huntley had been drinking boilermakers—"

"What?" Miss Withers interrupted blankly.

"Whiskey with a beer chaser. Anyway, he got a little tight—"

"Stinko!" corrected Midge. "I was there."

"So I broke our engagement, that's all," she concluded.

"You broke the engagement and the chicken-sandwich plate and all over his head because he suddenly went on the prowl for Helen Abbott," Midge reminded her, his voice a little louder than was necessary. "Helen was at the next table—she'd come as usual with Pat, and Lawn was tagging along. Pat decided to give kid sister a thrill by waltzing with her—

that was the time when her teeth were still in gold bands—and Huntley noticed that Helen was sitting all alone and looking very luscious in one of those strapless evening gowns. I was across the room with the Baldwins and the little Harper girl—"

"Bug-eyed and flat-chested," Adele cut in. "No wonder you were staring elsewhere—"

"Anyway," her husband continued dreamily, "jolly old Huntley insisted that you bring Helen over to your table, and pretty soon you got mad and flounced out of the place. Later on in the men's room Pat hung a right cross on Huntley's jaw and knocked him into the—"

"Midge Beale!"

"Into the middle of next week, I was going to say. That was how the romance started, really. A few weeks later Pat got himself selected into the Army. Helen carried the torch for a while and then I guess she got fed up with going out with only her father and kid sister all the time. Anyway, word got around that she and Huntley Cairns had been seen in town at the Stork and El Morocco, and pretty soon they were sitting in corners at parties studying *House and Garden*."

"Sealed-lips Beale," commented Adele.

"Well, it's common knowledge," Midge reminded her. "Relax, baby, nobody is going to think that you drowned Huntley Cairns because he got away from you three or four years ago."

"I'm afraid he's right," Miss Withers agreed in a somewhat disappointed tone. "There is still no apparent motive for anybody to kill Cairns—anybody but Pat Montague, that is. But I don't like to gamble on favorites, nor on extreme long shots either. Now what do you think of a nice in-between selection for the murderer—the commander, for instance, or Jed Nicolet?"

Midge laughed. "Sam Bennington might haul out a service pistol and blaze away at some poor unlucky guy that Ava had lured into her bedroom, but I can't see him drowning anyone. That's too subtle for Old Annapolis, Class of '26. And Jed Nicolet is a lawyer, and lawyers are too smart to commit murder. Besides, Jed is supposed to have a crush on Lawn, not Helen."

Miss Withers digested that. "I don't know about the rest of you," Adele spoke up suddenly, "but I'm going to have a snort. Purely medicinal, just to keep the top of my head from coming off. I feel like the hammers of hell, the ones they keep in the corner to pound toenails with. Where is it, Midge, *dear*?"

"There isn't anything in the house but the chartreuse," Midge told her.

"I tried and couldn't."

Miss Withers declined a pickup with thanks, and Adele tried the char-treuse and couldn't, either. The schoolteacher rose to her feet, deciding that this lead, which had looked so promising at first, was worked out. "There's just one question that I want to ask," she said. "Of course you don't have to answer, but it might help in clearing Pat Montague and putting an end to this investigation. Who, of all the people involved in the case, do you consider most capable of committing murder?"

"Lawn!" Adele said. "Lawn Abbott."

"But why?"

"Oh, I don't know. Except that she's such a strange, silent person, a sort of law unto herself. And she's dark and mysterious—sort of poison-ous, somehow. She did break up Helen and Pat's romance, I know she did. And Helen knows it too."

"And what did Lawn ever do that was on the wrong side of the ledger?"

"Aw, I don't like to ..." Adele shrugged. "Well, when she was in school, some swanky place near Boston, because that was when Thurlow Abbott still had some of his money, a poor little music teacher with a wife and three children got kicked out of his job for being caught kissing her. And she was supposed to have run away and got into some trouble and been in jail down south somewhere. Then a boy at Bar Harbor, two summers ago, tried to kill himself because she wouldn't run away with him. Besides"—and Adele made it clear that this was the crowning argument, the clincher—"besides, she hasn't any women friends, and she doesn't seem to want any!"

Miss Withers nodded. "Perhaps that is why Lawn didn't show up at her sister's housewarming, at least until the last minute. Well, I must be getting along. Thank you both for your help." She gathered her umbrella and pocketbook.

"That's all right. Drop in and listen to that new radio program, The Beale Family, any afternoon at five." Adele glared at her husband and then headed for the stairs.

Midge Beale walked to the door with Miss Withers. "Don't mind Adele, she's just hung over. Wonderful little wife—best housekeeper you ever saw. She can make a dollar do the work of three."

"How nice—and how loyal of you to say so."

He shrugged. "If my opinion is worth anything," Midge went on, "you won't get anywhere asking questions of Bennington and the rest of them. These local bigwigs stick together, and they're closemouthed. You should have seen the fuss Bennington and Nicolet made at the party when they thought I was eavesdropping on them in the library. And all they were doing was having a huddle over Huntley Cairns's taste in literature."

Miss Withers, about to head down the steps towards her taxi, stopped short. "Literature? You mean they were interested in his library?"

"That's right. And then they got started arguing with Mame Boad over whether or not I liked dogs. There was something Nicolet found in the far bookcase—something in a thin red book that he was going to read out loud, only Bennington stopped him because I was there. They were all hopped up about it."

"Thank you so much," Miss Withers said. "It doesn't seem pertinent at the moment, but you never can tell. I'm just collecting bits of cardboard now; I'm not trying to fit them into the puzzle yet." She frowned. "I wonder—no, I guess not. Good night, Mr. Beale."

She climbed into the taxi, hesitating before she gave the driver an address. She would have given anything for a talk with Pat Montague in the jail. His version of the fracas with Huntley Cairns in the Sands Point club men's room might be very interesting. But Pat was in no mood to see her, even if she could get by the barriers outside.

Or if she could only get into the Cairns house for an hour—that might lead to the uncovering of something. But the inspector had that staked out for himself. She would only be in the way.

" 'Sufficient unto the day is the evil thereof,' " she said.

The driver turned. "What say, lady?"

"The hotel, please," requested Miss Hildegarde Withers wearily.

She dined alone in the big hotel dining room, wondering, as always, how hotel chefs manage to make everything taste like canned salmon. Then she marched back to her cottage and unlocked the door.

"Merciful heavens!" cried the schoolteacher. "The room is a shambles!"

At any rate, shambles or not, it was evident that the place had been hastily but thoroughly searched in her absence. Cushions were askew on the davenport and on the chairs, the tacks along the edge of the carpet were all pulled out, and books had been taken out of their shelves and put back upside down, which made Miss Withers dizzy to look at. Even the cover of the aquarium had been removed and replaced so that it did not quite fit.

In the bedroom there were fewer signs of disturbance, and none at all in the kitchenette and bath. Nothing whatever seemed to be missing. Miss Withers sat down on the bed, frowning intently. What in the world could any one have imagined they would find here?

There was no sign that the lock had been forced, and the screens and windows were all in place, unmarred. "This lock will have to be replaced at once," Miss Withers decided, "or I shan't sleep a wink tonight, not a wink."

She picked up the phone and gave crisp and definite instructions to the man at the desk. He was very dubious about the possibility of getting a locksmith at this hour and on a Sunday, too, but she gave him what was usually referred to as a piece of her mind and hung up.

Miss Withers came into the living room, knelt down while she straightened the books, and then on an impulse she returned to the phone. "Get me the local police station," she insisted.

The night clerk, evidently a very uneasy and suspicious type, tried to find out why she wanted the police. "Never you mind, young man!" she snapped. "Just get the police. I want to talk to Inspector Oscar Piper. I'm going to report that my cottage was broken into this afternoon and turned topsy-turvy—"

"Yes, I know," sounded a quiet voice behind her. She whirled, to see the inspector himself standing in the front doorway.

"Oscar!" she cried. "I was just trying to get hold of you! I don't understand. Has this vandalism already been reported?"

He came into the room, looking slightly sheepish. "Well, I know all about it," the inspector said slowly. "You see, Hildegarde, I ordered it done."

She stared at him balefully. "Do I understand you to say—"

"I sent Sergeant Fischer over here," Piper confessed as he sank uninvited into her most comfortable chair. "Relax, and I'll tell you about it. You see, we were hunting for Huntley Cairns's wristwatch."

She blinked. "Well, why hunt for it here—was the light better or something? I assure you that I haven't set up as a fence."

"The watch was missing," said Piper wearily. "It's one of those jobs set in solid crystal that tell the hour and the day and the year. His wife gave it to him when they were married, and we had to make sure that young Montague hadn't taken it off the body and then secreted it here when he knew he was going to be arrested."

"But you didn't find it, did you?"

The inspector looked at her, a shy leprechaunish smile lighting his face. "Oh, sure we found it. But not here. They finally got around to draining the swimming pool this afternoon, and it was buried in the mud and stuff at the bottom. Here it is, still ticking."

He showed her the tiny, glittering thing. One link in the flexible platinum band was broken. "It's a clue, anyway," the inspector pronounced.

"The law," said Miss Hildegarde Withers, "puts a great deal too much faith in tangible things, such as clues and weapons and alibis, and not enough in the imponderables. Whose brilliant mind was it, by the way, that leaped to the conclusion that Pat Montague might have removed the wristwatch from his victim before drowning him? Is it now the official police theory that this was robbery, with murder only an accidental by-product?"

The inspector looked uncomfortable. "We have to eliminate every possibility," he said defensively. "Young Montague might have known that the watch was a wedding present from Helen to her husband, and in a flareup of jealousy—"

"Never in a million years, Oscar Piper." Miss Withers handed back the watch. "What else did the majesty of the law uncover up at the scene of the crime, if I'm not too inquisitive?"

The inspector took out a long greenish-brown cigar, sniffed it, and put it away in his pocket again. "It's a funny setup," he admitted. "When I first arrived at the Cairns place I could see that nobody was especially anxious to cooperate. The old man is a phony, like most actors. The widow is supposed to be crying her eyes out with grief, but if you ask me, she's more scared than sorrowful. The kid sister doesn't care a whoop in hell for anybody or anything, or at least that's the impression she wants to give—but she hangs around, all the same, trying to kibitz on what we're doing. The servants are pulling the old, old gag—they pretend they don't quite understand and retreat into a mess of 'Yassuhs' and 'Ah sho'ly don' know nuffins.' "

"Defense mechanism," the schoolteacher put in. "In looking over the place, didn't you stumble on anything—anything unusual?"

He scowled. "We went all through the place, particularly Cairns's desk in the library, but we didn't find much except receipted bills. The house cost twice as much as he had expected, but I guess he expected that. Cairns's closet was full of super deluxe elevator shoes, guaranteed to make a man two inches taller overnight—"

"I wonder," Miss Withers observed, "why people laugh so much at someone who tried to make himself look taller with special shoes, or younger with hair dye or a toupee, or slimmer with a corset. Because, basically, we all want to appear at our best."

"Ugh," said the inspector. "Well, now you know about as much as I do. Except that in Helen Cairns's closet she kept a weekend case packed and ready. We thought we had something there for a minute, but she explained that she had packed it six months ago, after she'd had an argument with her husband about plans for the new house, and she had never unpacked. Nothing else incriminating around the place."

"There wouldn't be," said the schoolteacher. "This is an odd sort of murder, Oscar, and it's not according to the formula at all. I can't help feeling that either the wrong person was murdered, or it was at the wrong time, or—or something!"

He looked at her. "Come clean, Hildegarde. What have you been up to?"

She told him sketchily about the call on the Beale family. "I can't help wondering," she said, "if there could be any tie-up between what Midge Beale told me and something that happened about six weeks ago, when I first came here. I had a call from a little group of upstanding, public-spirited local citizens—Dr. Radebaugh, Mrs. Boad, and Commander and Mrs. Bennington. They at first gave me the impression that they were collecting for a home for wayward girls or something, but finally they admitted that they wanted me to do a job of confidential sleuthing for them. My reputation as a meddler had preceded me, I imagine via Mr. Nicolet, who remembered our day in court. At any rate, they wouldn't tell me what they wanted me to do until I promised to help them, and I wasn't willing to buy a pig in a poke. Besides, I had only just given you my solemn promise not to mix into police affairs, so I told them that I had retired, or reformed, or something, and sent them on about their business. I'd give anything now to know what it was that they wanted."

The inspector pointed out reasonably that nobody could have been after her to solve the Cairns murder six weeks before it happened. As a matter of fact, it was clear that nobody had planned this murder ahead of time because nobody could know that Huntley Cairns would be so excited about his new swimming pool that he would leave his guests in the house and rush out for a quick dip—especially when it was drizzling. "This murder," he concluded, "was done on the cuff—on the spur of the moment."

"There is always the possibility," Miss Withers mused, "that the local committee, or some Machiavellian member of it, contemplated a murder and wanted to get me on their side beforehand—or to send me off on some wild-goose chase."

"Relax, Hildegarde! Nobody ever has to send you on a wild-goose chase. You go by yourself. And don't worry. If you think it's important I'll find out what it was that the local committee had on its mind." He picked up his hat and started for the door.

"With a rack and thumbscrew, Oscar—because I have a feeling that they have, as you say, 'clammed up.' On second thought, the rack and thumbscrew would be a very good idea."

"I won't even have to use a rubber hose," he promised, and took his departure.

CHAPTER SEVEN

Next morning Miss Hildegarde Withers arose early and at once set about removing from her little cottage all traces of the police search, putting everything back into its spick-and-span—though slightly prim—order. This accomplished, she sat herself down with a pot of coffee and a plate of molasses cookies to study the morning papers.

The local sheet, unfortunately, had almost nothing at all. "Tragic Accident Mars Cairns Party" was the head. The news story gave the impression that the police investigation into Huntley Cairns's death was a mere formality and that a verdict of accidental death would most certainly result from the coroner's inquest, scheduled for today.

So Knight's County still clung to the archaic "crowner's quest" instead of trusting to a medical examiner! That would make things a bit harder all around, the school ma'am decided. So she put the Shoreham *Standard* aside and took up the metropolitan sheets.

It was immediately clear to Miss Withers that the heat was on. The Manhattan dailies hadn't been able to get much more out of the inspector than had she last evening. But to make up for the paucity of news, there was a good deal of art, some of it obviously dug up out of the files and the rest being photographs of the Cairns house, the gardens, swimming pool, etcetera.

There were photographs, some of them three or four years old, according to the hat and dress styles, of most of the principals in the case. "Wife in Pool Mystery with Other Man" was an old shot of Helen with Pat

Montague at Café Society Uptown. Thurlow Abbott was in the picture too—which must have been the reason it was taken, for in those days he had still been remembered as a celebrity. There was also "Pool Widow with Husband in Happier Days," which was Helen and Huntley Cairns down in the Village at Asti's. Then there was a shot of Helen, Lawn Thurlow Abbott, and Huntley Cairns in the Easter parade outside St. Patrick's on the Avenue, and another picture of Lawn, looking very like a defiant ghost, tied up with the scandal about the boy at Bar Harbor. The original caption, reprinted here, was "Deep-freeze Girl Jilts Social Registerite—He Tries Gas."

Miss Withers decided that Lawn looked scared to death, and why wouldn't she? And she'd just had that unhappy experience with the music teacher, too! Remembering certain music teachers of her acquaintance, and social registerites, too, the schoolteacher was inclined to be a little more sympathetic towards Lawn than her own friends and family seemed to be.

There was a column which seemed to be a biography of the dead man. "Cairns, president and founder of Cairns Associates, the extremely successful public-relations consultants with offices in the Jollity Building, numbered among his clients some of the most prominent figures in the theatrical world, both in motion pictures and in radio."

There were, however, no statements from any of those prominent radio and movie personalities, which struck Miss Withers as a bit unusual. She turned to the stories on the crime itself. Most of the papers went as far as they dared in hinting at the triangle between Pat Montague, Huntley Cairns, and Helen. They intimated that, while at the moment Montague was held only on charges of suspicion of homicide, it would probably be merely a matter of hours before he would be booked and held for the grand jury on the charge of first-degree murder. Miss Withers was of the private opinion that for once the press was right.

Montague had her to thank for that. Well, it was now or never, if she was to do anything in his behalf. She gathered herself together, clamped upon her head a hat which somewhat resembled a frigate under full sail, and took off. Ten minutes later her taxicab deposited her at the gateway of the Cairns house.

"You want I should wait for you like yesterday?" the driver wanted to know.

She thought and then shook her head. "No, thank you. I may be some time—I hope." She headed for the front door, to find Officer Ray Lunney guarding it, sprawled out in a bright green-and-yellow canvas deck chair.

"Nobody home, ma'am," he announced importantly. "They're all down to the inquest, even the jigaboo servants."

"The *what*?"

"The jigs—I mean niggers."

"The word is 'Negro,'" corrected Miss Hildegarde Withers firmly. "And when a lady is speaking to you, young man, you might have the courtesy to stand up. By the way, are you the heavy-handed lout who searched my cottage yesterday afternoon?"

Lunney blinked and stood up. "Why—why, no, ma'am. That was the sarge. He's down at the inquest. If you want to look in, it's being held at the Magee Funeral Home on Middle Street. It'll likely take all day, unless they adjourn it," he added hopefully.

"Thank you so much," said the schoolteacher. "I'm afraid that I have too much else on my mind." She hesitated. "It must be very boring for you, officer, to be stuck up here when so much is going on down at the inquest."

He blinked and nodded. "Especially since I was one of the first to answer the alarm after Searles phoned in. But Sergeant Fischer is testifying for us both." It was evident that she had touched on a sore spot, and Miss Withers decided to probe a bit further.

"I should think they'd want your testimony," she said.

He flushed. "They say I done too much talking already. But all I said to the reporters that come out from the city was that Joe Searles was a criminal type, that's all."

"Really, officer? Tell me, how do you spot a criminal type?"

Lunney brightened. "Well, it's like this. A criminal type is like when it's late at night on a lonely street and a cop is walking along and he sees somebody coming. You follow me?"

"At a distance, yes."

"Well, the regular citizen, Joe Doakes, who's been to lodge meeting or working late or whatever, he goes along on the brightest side of the street, and he's probably whistling out loud to himself for company and maybe to keep his spirits up. When he sees a cop on the corner he feels good about it and he says, 'Evenin', officer,' or something. But the criminal type, he slouches along on the dark side of the street, maybe talking to himself in a low mumble, and when he sees a cop he walks faster and keeps his face down so he can't be seen so easy."

"I see. And Searles is the latter type?"

Officer Lunney nodded. "I seen him, night after night, when I used to walk a beat. He just don't like cops, and when a person don't like cops he's got a reason not to like cops."

"It all sounds sensible to me," Miss Withers told him. "And it certainly sheds a new light on the character of one of the principals in this case. Have you had a chance to transmit this to your superiors?"

Lunney shook his head. "Sheriff Vinge, he's playing hands off this case. Too much local dynamite involved, especially for election year. That's why he called for a hotshot homicide man from New York, who throws his weight around plenty. That's why I'm stuck here. According to the inspector, somebody always has to stay on duty any place where there's a murder, for a couple of days, anyway. He says that's the way they do it in New York."

"Imagine that!" sympathized Miss Withers. "Well, good morning, officer." She headed for the highway again, followed by shouted directions as to the shortest way to get to Middle Street and the inquest.

Then Officer Lunney sank back into the deck chair, so that the hot June sun bit into the underside of his jaw, the only portion of his anatomy which he had never been able to get satisfactorily tanned. He lighted a cigarette, stuck it into his mouth at an angle, and was a perfect picture of repose some time later when a police sedan rolled quietly into the driveway and stopped.

Inspector Oscar Piper swung out, carefully not slamming the door, and came up to the front entrance, walking on the balls of his feet. His face wore an expression of hopeful inquiry.

Lunney opened his eyes, nodded meaningly, and started to speak, but the inspector only scowled and pressed a finger against his mouth. He soundlessly asked, "How many?"

The officer held up one stubby forefinger and would have risen had not the inspector shaken his head and gone on into the house alone, making no noise whatever in the process. In the side pocket of his coat he felt the sag of a police-positive, borrowed from Sheriff Vinge for the occasion. The inspector was not in the habit of packing a pistol, his theory being that a cop who couldn't handle his job without a heater didn't know his business. But there were exceptions to everything.

Piper tiptoed along the hall, through the big modern drawing room, and was about to mount the stairs when he thought he heard a sound—a mouselike, shushing ghost of a sound—in the direction of the library. He went silently and grimly across the thick broadloom carpet, through the library doors, and then stopped stock still.

"Judas Priest in a bathtub!" he roared. "Don't you ever stay home?"

Miss Hildegarde Withers, who had been carefully studying a row of books on the bottom shelf, straightened up with a small squeak of alarm. "Oscar! What in the world are you doing here?"

"I'm here because everybody thought I'd be at the inquest, and I had a sort of trap baited, with that fool of a Lunney half-asleep out front and the rear door open and unguarded, hoping somebody …" He stopped, shaking his head angrily. "Why do I have to explain it to you? You'd better tell me why you're housebreaking."

"I was just looking around," Miss Withers said.

"So I see." The inspector nodded towards the strewn papers around the big library desk, the half-open, rifled drawers, the overturned wastebasket.

"I hope, Oscar, that you don't think I'm responsible for that mess!"

He shook his head wearily. "Of course not. But you're responsible for scaring away whoever *was* searching this room!"

"Then," retorted Miss Withers triumphantly, "Pat Montague is cleared. Because if he's in jail he couldn't have sneaked in here—"

"I didn't say it was him. He could have sent somebody—"

"But why would he need to do that? He was never inside the house, so he couldn't have left his cuff buttons or anything behind. Besides, the only friends he has are the people who live in this house, and Helen and Lawn wouldn't need to sneak in to do any searching. They live here."

"I still say it's a simple triangle," the inspector insisted wearily. "Just two men who wanted the same woman. It's ABC."

Miss Withers shook her head so hard that the frigate almost let loose a spinnaker. "No, no, Oscar! It isn't a triangle; it's a much more complicated figure, a pentacle or a pentagon or something. It would all be very much simpler if I could find that red book—only maybe it's just a red herring. Anyway, young Beale overheard enough in here to realize that Commander Bennington and Nicolet and Mrs. Boad were very excited about a book in a red jacket—"

"That's easy," Piper decided. "It's natural that the local gentry were interested in finding out what sort of neighbor they were going to have— whether Huntley Cairns would fit into the dog-loving, horse-show, country-club set or not. Go ahead and look for the book with the red jacket that Nicolet was so excited about. Ten to one it's something with some bearing on Cairns's tastes or background—something that proves he once played polo at Meadow Brook or won a blue ribbon with a bird dog."

Miss Withers sniffed. "It's not as easy as all that. Besides, I have been looking. I've peeked into every book with a red jacket in this library, and I don't see anything for any one to get excited about. Here they are—look for yourself, and if you can see what interested Jed Nicolet you have better eyes than I have."

The inspector obediently took up the volumes one by one. "*Six Who Boil While the Lentils Pass*, the stirring story of a man who was allergic to himself, by somebody named Weatherby." He ruffled the pages. "Nothing here." He picked up the next one. "*Art of the Dance*, by Señor Pablo Miltberg. *Old Man Gordy's System*—or how to make money at the greyhound races. That couldn't be it—or could it?"

Miss Withers thought not. There were no notes or enclosures in any of the volumes, no scribbled messages or marginal writings. "It must be something else," she insisted.

There was only one other volume which by any stretch of the imagination could have been said to have a red jacket, and that was something called *Sea-Rimes*, a little book of outdoor, masculine verse illustrated by the author, whose tastes had run to ships and storms and spouting whales. "That simply cannot be it," Miss Withers complained. "Oscar, I'm afraid that the person who searched this room took the book we want with him."

Piper doubted it and said so. "If he'd found it in the shelves he wouldn't have torn up the desk. Besides, I can see that there's no gap in the shelves. The books are crowded, not scattered, and they just fill up the cases."

It was, Miss Withers had to admit, a point well taken. Not even the schoolteacher could visualize the shadowy intruder bringing along a volume to substitute for the one he intended to take. Of course, he might have shoved the books along to fill the gap, but he really hadn't had time for that.

"Well, Hildegarde, is there anything else you'd like to look for before we get out of here?"

The sarcasm went over her head. "There is," said Hildegarde Withers. "I'd like to look for the murderer, or whoever it was that was here. Because he's probably lurking somewhere in the house, waiting for a chance to continue his job of ransacking the place."

"Okay," the inspector said. "Let's go." And he searched the Cairns house from top to bottom, Miss Withers tagging along at his heels. But while he was pulling open closet doors and looking under beds, the schoolteacher turned her sharp scrutiny on the rooms themselves, the furniture, the personal possessions scattered around. It was, she felt, necessary for her to know Huntley Cairns and the rest of his household better than she did at the moment, and this was one way.

Her first impression of Huntley Cairns's room was that it was aggressively masculine, interior-decorator masculine, with heavy oak furniture, sporting prints and *La Vie Parisienne* pictures on the walls, and an unusually large collection of shaving lotions, hair remedies, deodorants, and the like. He also had three straight razors, three electric shavers, and one battered silver safety which seemed to have carried most of the burden. There was a large framed photograph of Helen on the bureau but no other sign of her in the room.

Helen's domain, consisting of bedroom, dressing-room, and bath, was surprisingly simple, the schoolteacher thought. There was but one bottle of perfume, and that nearly empty. Too, there were fewer dresses in the closet than Huntley Cairns's wife would be expected to possess. A large floppy doll, reminiscent of Josephine Baker, sat at the head of the bed, and nearby was a little bookcase filled with travel books, cookbooks, several eyewitness accounts of the war, and some sentimental poetry. None of the books had a red jacket, or any jacket at all, for that matter.

To Miss Withers's disappointment, there were no letters, no knick-knacks, but that was to be expected when one realized that the family had only just moved into the place and hadn't had time to accumulate the usual flotsam and jetsam. "She hasn't even a mink coat," Miss Withers said. "I don't think that Helen made the most of her opportunities." She briefly studied the weekend case which Helen had kept packed on a shelf at the rear of the closet, but there was nothing in it except a few light rayon and cotton dresses, underwear, and two pairs of nylons.

"Come on." the inspector urged. "What do you expect to find that the police haven't found?"

"I won't know until I find it," she told him. "But, Oscar, how odd of the girl to pack a bag during a family quarrel and then forget to unpack it!"

"There is," said the inspector, "no telling what any woman will do." He led the way on into Thurlow Abbott's room, small but luxurious, and crammed with photographs, old clipping books, mash letters, and other relics of his theatrical past. There was a bottle of cognac tucked away in a riding boot in the closet, another in the bottom bureau drawer beneath his winter underwear, and a third stuck in behind a cabinet photograph of himself in hussar's uniform which stood on the chest of drawers.

"He certainly takes no chances of being caught in a drought," Miss Withers observed.

Last of all the master bedrooms, whose windows opened on the balcony, was Lawn's room, but by this time the inspector was getting so impatient that Miss Withers had only time to gain the impression that, for all her straightforward simplicity, the girl did herself rather well. There were silk sheets on the bed, the bedside table had a portable radio-phonograph with a great many records, and the pictures were reproductions from the Museum of Modern Art of Picasso's Clown and two or three of Marie Laurencin's dreamy pre-Raphaelite girls.

High on the chest of drawers sat a worn, furry monkey grinning down enigmatically, and beneath it was a silver candlestick well guttered with wax, a large incense burner, and a dozen or so bottles of perfume. Miss Withers's personal tastes ran to rose and violet toilet water, but she realized that most of these scents were rare and expensive, almost unobtainable now.

While the inspector fidgeted impatiently she took a peek into the closet. It appeared that Lawn's wardrobe was largely confined to evening dresses, slacks, and riding-habits. Along one wall was a rank of riding-boots, jodhpur shoes, and fragile high-heeled slippers, but a pair of rubber-soled sneakers appeared to have received the most wear.

A wispy scarf and panties of blazing crimson were drying on a hanger. That would be the bathing suit that Lawn had worn in her private investigation of the pool yesterday morning.

A little reluctantly Miss Withers followed the inspector out of the room. "That's the works," he said. "Except for the servants' room over the kitchen."

"What, no nursery?"

"Cairns probably figured he had family enough with his wife's father and sister on his hands."

Miss Withers had a quick look at the servants' room and bath, which was so neat and impersonal that it might have served as a model bedroom in a department-store exhibit. There was a chessboard set up on the bedside table, an armful of fresh red roses in a big vase on the bureau, and a tiny shelf of books which included John Donne, Walter Pater, George Crabbe, Emily Post, and Countee Cullen. None of the books had a red jacket.

"So that's that," said the inspector.

"We've settled one thing, at least," the schoolteacher announced. "From none of the bedroom windows, not even Helen's, is the swimming pool visible. The bathhouse cuts off the view."

The inspector said he already knew that. None of the guests at the party could have known that Huntley Cairns was alone at the pool. They went downstairs again, came finally into the kitchen, where an elderly man in filthy overalls was placidly making himself a sandwich out of canapes left over from the party, putting a whole slab of them between two slices of bread.

"Searles!" cried the inspector. "What are you doing here?"

"Eating," said Searles. He kept on.

"You're supposed to be down at the inquest."

"I was down to the inquest," admitted the gardener wearily. "I was the first witness called, and when they got through with me I came back to work. Nobody said anything about my being fired, and gardens gotta be watered, whether folks die or not. More I see of people, more I like plants, anyway."

Questioned further by the inspector, Searles emphatically denied seeing anybody or hearing anybody prowling around the place. But he had been busy turning on sprinklers.

"And don't go looking at me fishy-eyed because I'm in the house," the old man went on. He showed a key. "I have the run of the place because it's my job to keep fresh flowers in all the rooms. I'm supposed to have my lunch, too, but with the help gone, I had to make my own."

The inspector took Miss Withers's arm and showed her into the dining room. "That's reasonable enough," he said to her. "No point in getting the old man riled up—he's plenty sore at everybody for being arrested. You know how it is."

"Gardens do have to be watered," admitted the schoolteacher thoughtfully. "But, Oscar—"

"Save it," the inspector told her. "I want to get back down to the inquest before it's over and done with. Come on, I'll give you a ride home—and will you please stay there and keep from throwing monkey wrenches?"

Miss Withers didn't answer him. She pulled away, heading towards the library. "Just a minute, Oscar. I have an idea—a wonderful idea. It'll only take a minute."

Grumbling, he followed her into the library. "What's this, a retake?"

"Listen, Oscar. It was late in the afternoon when Mr. Beale and the others were in here—"

"Suppose it was?"

"The windows face to the east. It must have been quite dark, so the lights would have been on, wouldn't they?"

"Suppose they were?"

Without answering she pulled the venetian blinds, drew down the shades, and turned on all the lights. "Now!" cried Miss Withers. "Don't you see, Oscar? Artificial light brings out colors that aren't there by daylight. A book jacket that looked yellowish-orange by day could look red at night. We will have to look carefully—there! I see one now!"

She pounced upon a thin volume on one of the middle shelves and then stopped, her eyes clouded with disappointment. The reddish-orange jacket bore the title *Oriental Moments* and a drawing of a well-proportioned Chinese dancing girl without any clothes on, but the book inside turned out to be something else entirely. It was *Fitz on Contract—300 Hands Analyzed.*

"And if that's a clue," remarked the inspector unpleasantly, "then I'm a monkey's uncle. Unless of course you think that somebody drowned Huntley Cairns because he led from a king or left his partner in a secondary suit."

Miss Hildegarde Withers stared at the treatise on contract bridge for a few moments, and then she slowly replaced the misleading wrapper and shoved the book back into its place on the shelf.

"Oscar," she said, "the trouble is that we don't know enough about the victim, his background, and all that sort of thing."

"Don't we? We know that he flunked out of Dartmouth for trying to buy a list of examination questions from a French instructor, that he lost half the money his father left him trying to beat the stock market in 1931 and '32, that he worked more than a year as account executive for a radio advertising agency and then set up in business for himself—"

"And immediately hit the jackpot! He was either smarter than we think or luckier than he had any business to be. Sudden success such as his must have been achieved at the risk of stepping on somebody else's toes— business rivals, that sort of thing."

The inspector didn't think so. "We had a man go up to Cairns Associates and take a look-see. He reported everything okay—Cairns seems to have been himself and the associates too. According to his office staff, he had the habit of working late about one night a week with a string of models and chorus girls, but that isn't unusual for a man whose home life is on the frigid side."

Miss Withers shrugged. "Perhaps I'm wrong," she admitted. She was very, very meek as she followed the inspector towards the front door, but far back in a corner of her mind an idea was beginning to take shape.

CHAPTER EIGHT

Down in the town of Shoreham the crowd was pushing out of the funeral home into the sunshine. One or another of the photographers darted out to get a shot of Helen Abbott Cairns, a handkerchief to her face, as her father hurried her towards the car.

The reporters yapped like a kennel of hounds: "May we quote you as saying …" "Is it true that …" "Does this verdict …" But their cries were terminated by the slamming of the limousine door and the roar of its motor.

Beneath the great evergreen which shaded the doorway Jed Nicolet stood idly tapping a cigarette against the back of his hand. Commander Bennington came up beside him. "Well!" said the Navy man.

Nicolet nodded. "Deceased came to his death at the hands of person or persons unknown. Only we know, don't we, Sam?"

"Stop talking like that, you young fool!"

"Well, don't we?"

"They're still holding that soldier," said the commander huffily. "He certainly had a motive, being crazy in love with Helen. And the opportunity too."

Nicolet shook his head. "Not Montague. That's why I mixed into it Saturday night. He isn't going to take the rap."

"Bilge!" Bennington stuck his lower lip out far enough so that he could have gazed down upon it. "They have no real case against him, not now,

75

anyway. They'll have to let him go for lack of evidence; you're a lawyer and you know that. I don't see anything to be gained by talking, do you?"

"It depends on where you're sitting," Jed Nicolet pointed out. "Not from the standpoint of Mrs. Boad, or the doctor, or you. Or me, for that matter. I was an accessory before the fact; I suppose I might as well be one after. All the same, it's not too nice to know that one of your friends, one of the people you play bridge and tennis with and meet at the Marine Room for dinner every Saturday, is a murderer."

"But as long as we don't know which one—" Bennington suggested. "Besides, Cairns had it coming to him."

"You'd feel differently," Nicolet told him, "if Pat Montague were on trial for his life, which he very likely will be. Are you for keeping silent even then?"

Bennington didn't say anything. Mrs. Boad and Trudy were coming towards them. He looked off, saw his wife, and bowed out. "Ava's waiting," he called out over his shoulder. "We'll talk about it later, won't we, Jed?"

"Such a fuss!" Mame Boad remarked after a moment. "And all over practically nothing! It's such a shame that Huntley Cairns has all that money. If he were poor this would have been written off as an accidental death."

"If he'd been poor he wouldn't have had a swimming pool to get drowned in," Jed reminded her.

Mrs. Boad snorted. "I must be running along—Trudy has to get to the hairdresser's. Do come up for dinner one night this week and we'll talk about it then. But I still insist that the whole thing is crystal-clear. That Abbott girl's testimony clinched it. Cairns died an accidental death by getting caught on that metal hook, or whatever it was, down underwater in the pool."

"In spite of the fact that the man could barely swim on the surface?"

Mame Boad said there was no telling what some people would do, and flounced off. Jed threw away his cigarette and started after them and then was halted by a jovial hail from Dr. Radebaugh. "Drop you anywhere, Jed?"

Nicolet shook his head. "I'm walking back. I want to think. This setup is all wrong."

"You're doing too much thinking," the doctor advised him. "It isn't good for you—makes for ulcers and things. Better come up to my office and have a checkup."

He climbed into his roadster, and Jed started off along the sidewalk.

There was still plenty wrong with the setup. Wrong because of many things, but chiefly because of Huntley Cairns, who now lay back inside that funeral parlor in an expensive casket with real silver handles, unwept, unhonored, and unsung. Most definitely unwept.

Jed walked slowly back down town, pausing at the Elite Florists to order a suitable floral tribute for the funeral. He wondered if it was in good taste to send a corsage of orchids to the widow. Probably not, he decided, and chose two dozen waxy-white Frau Karl Druschki roses. On second thought he ordered the orchids sent to Lawn.

Up at the salmon-pink house on the hill, Miss Hildegarde Withers was just being aided into the police sedan by the inspector when a taxi pulled up and deposited Lawn Abbott. She stopped short, staring, and then came forward, looking stranger and paler than ever in the navy-blue suit which she had worn as suitable for inquests and funerals. "Just exactly what is going on here?" she demanded bluntly.

"Er—you see—" began Miss Withers.

"I get it!" Lawn said. "Miss Withers, you're being arrested, aren't you?" She whirled on the inspector. "What's it for? I demand to know!"

He stared at her, straight-faced. "Now, if you're really demanding you may as well know that this lady's been laying herself open to a charge of breaking and entering. Or illegal entry, anyway."

"Is that it?" Lawn Abbott drew herself up to her full height, which was slightly over five feet, including her heels. "Then let me tell you something, mister policeman. You can't hold Miss Withers on any such charge as that. She had every right to be in the house!"

"Just why?" asked the inspector very gravely.

"Because I asked her to! Only yesterday morning I called her into the case because I could see what a botch the regular police were making of it. If she came inside she was only there at my request, trying to straighten out this muddle! Now, let's see you arrest her and make it stick!"

The inspector, containing himself with difficulty, bowed. "Under the circumstances I haven't any choice," he admitted. "Miss Withers, you have been sprung, and how!" He winked at her behind Lawn's back.

"I certainly have, haven't I?" murmured the schoolteacher, a little taken aback at the girl's intense partisanship.

Lawn grasped her hand. "Please come on back in. I want to talk to you."

"I think maybe I'll come too," suggested Inspector Piper wickedly.

"You'll come with a search warrant tucked in your hot little hand, and not without it!" Lawn drew Miss Withers towards the front door, pausing to glare at Officer Lunney sprawled in the deck chair.

Once inside, Miss Withers shook her head. "Very kind of you—but, child, aren't you afraid of making enemies sometimes? You were rather short with the inspector, and in front of one of his subordinates too."

"Oh, dear. That's a knack I seem to have," Lawn admitted ruefully. "For making un-friends. I'm always getting into trouble because I say what I mean and what I think—in a world full of people who live by double talk." She led the way into the living room and threw herself down on a big divan, relaxing immediately as a cat on a cushion.

"I suppose," she said, "you think I'm an odd person. Maybe I am. Maybe you're a bit odd too. I guess I shouldn't have rushed out of your place yesterday—I had no business to have hurt feelings. But please tell me what's going on and what's going to happen. I left the inquest early when I saw the way it was going, but Helen and Father will be along shortly. We haven't much time."

"It is later than you think," the schoolteacher agreed. "They used to inscribe that on sundials, so it must be true."

"I'm truly sorry that I blew up yesterday," Lawn repeated. She bit thoughtfully at the tip of her right forefinger. "I guess I'm just the moody type. But I'd just had a scene with Helen and Father. I can't stand my family, you see, and they can't stand me. Never mind that—I hear that you are doing your level best to get Pat out of jail, and I want to know all about it, and how I can help. By the way, if it's a question of money—"

"Dear me, no," Miss Withers assured her. "Snooping is for me a labor of love, and I don't want to lose my amateur standing at this late date. As for the progress I'm making, all I can say is that I've tripped over a number of threads. I don't know just where they lead, except that they do not lead towards Pat Montague. If he had had murder in his heart he wouldn't have come along the highway in broad daylight to crash a party he hadn't been invited to. He'd have sneaked in after dark, with an Army pistol or a hand grenade or something—"

"You mentioned *threads*," Lawn reminded her.

"I did. One thread seems to lead to a group of outstanding local citizens who made a mysterious proposition to me some weeks ago. Another indicates your gardener, who may not be a murderer but who takes it upon himself to water lawns and flowerbeds in the heat of the day, which, according to the best horticultural authorities, is simply not done. A third is tangled up with the personality and background of Cairns himself—how he managed to make a million dollars or so in three years, and just what sort of public relations he was mixed up in. He doesn't seem the type, somehow—"

"To make money, you mean? But everybody's been making money the last three years."

"Every one fortunate enough not to wear a uniform, you mean. However, I was referring to Cairns's personality. He isn't like any public-relations man I ever knew. They are usually ex-reporters or disappointed writers. Cairns was in his late thirties, which means that he came to maturity in the between-war era. I would expect any publicity or public-relations man to have some manuscript poetry in the back of his desk, or the first draft of the great American novel. At the very least there should be some worn volumes of James Branch Cabell and Floyd Dell and Ronald Firbank somewhere in his library."

Lawn nodded. "Huntley was different." She pointed. "You know, I wouldn't like to admit it to everybody, but every book in the library in there was bought in bulk from a dealer in town. He got what they call publishers' remainders. Those are the ones that they can't sell in the ordinary way. He didn't care, as long as they filled up the shelves. Neither did Helen; she's no reader. If there isn't any dancing or bridge or anything, she just goes to sleep."

"Very sensible of her, in a way. But to return to my threads—the last one has to do with a book in a red jacket, a book that seems to have mysteriously disappeared from the library and which somebody must have been searching for at the time I dropped in."

Miss Withers was watching Lawn's face very closely, but the girl only looked blank at the mention of the book. "I don't understand," she said. "Who'd want to take one of the books? I told you they were all remainders, at ten or twenty cents apiece. So there isn't much chance of a first-folio Shakespeare or a Gutenberg Bible or anything. I mean, there couldn't be anything of the slightest value."

"I doubt very much," observed Miss Hildegarde Withers, "if this murder was committed for money. After all, nobody benefits financially but your sister, and she had everything already."

"Everything," Lawn agreed softly. "Except Pat Montague."

"But, child, didn't you indicate yesterday that your sister had never loved anything except herself?"

The girl smiled wryly. "There's love—and then there's wanting somebody because he's all the things your husband isn't. Because he's tall and good looking and dances well and is a sort of war hero and represents the things you've lost. As I told you, Helen is emotionally immature."

"In your opinion, would Helen have run away with Pat Montague if he'd asked her to?"

Lawn thought about that for some time. Then she shook her head. "She's too conventional. Besides, Pat wouldn't have asked her to—not after he'd actually seen for himself that she was really and truly married to somebody else. Pat's a poet, really, but he's the soul of honor."

"Too honorable to hold a successful rival under water until he drowned, at any rate?" Miss Withers nodded. "By the way, I almost forgot to ask. Just what was the final autopsy report?"

"What everyone expected. The autopsy surgeon backed up everything that Harry Radebaugh had diagnosed Saturday night, just after it happened. Huntley died from something called 'syncope,' which means he strangled all at once, from shock."

"Did you testify?"

"Just about the snag at the bottom of the pool. I don't know how much stock they put in what I said. I tried to point out some other things to them, but they cut me off short. I guess they thought I was just trying to protect my sister and her guilty lover, which is a laugh. The whole police theory in this case is ridiculous. Come on, I'll prove it to you—"

Lawn leaped suddenly to her feet and drew Miss Withers out through the rear of the house, down the steps, across the patio, and down the path which led around the bathhouse. Before them lay the big concrete-lined hole in the ground which had once been the swimming pool, with only a few puddles of murky water at the bottom.

"It was here that they found him," Lawn said, pointing towards a corner of the pool at the deep end, the widest part of the oval. Peering down, Miss Withers could see the exit of the drainpipe, and by squinting a little she fancied that she could make out the jagged bit of metal which had caught and held the body of Huntley Cairns.

"Dear, dear!" she said.

"Now, look, Miss Withers," Lawn said abruptly. "Do you know how long a garden rake is?"

"When I was a girl," the schoolteacher said, "there used to be a riddle about how long is a piece of string, but I forget the answer."

"This is no riddle. Because garden rakes are all approximately the same length. Wait a minute." The girl disappeared around the corner of the building and in a moment was back with an ordinary rake. She held it erect on the tiles so that the teeth came almost but not quite to her forehead. "You see? They don't make rakes any longer than this. The one the police took away as Exhibit A was just like this. And yet Pat is supposed to have murdered Huntley by holding him under with a rake, like this."

Lawn took the tool to the edge of the swimming pool, reached down with it as far as she could. "You see? The pool was just ten feet deep here, and the rake handle is barely five. If you allow a couple of feet for the width of the body, then the murderer must still have reached down a good three feet into the water in order to hook Huntley's shorts on to that projecting bit of metal."

The schoolteacher inclined her head gravely. "Your mathematics seem correct," she admitted.

"Well, then! Pat's sleeves were only wet a little at the wrist when I let him out of that dressing room Saturday night. Jed Nicolet can testify to the same thing because he saw Pat in the bar only a little while later."

"And how about Searles's sleeves?"

"I didn't see him. But it wouldn't matter, even if he was dripping to the shoulder, because he did most of the work hauling the body out, remember. He must have had to reach down as far as he could to hook the rake—" She stopped, biting her lip. "What a grisly business this is!"

Miss Withers was inclined to agree with her. They headed back for the house by way of the toolshed so Lawn could replace the rake. The flagged path led them almost to the kitchen door, and then the schoolteacher stopped short, pointing a lean finger. "What's that?"

Lawn hesitated. "It looks like Helen's white bathing suit. I guess Beulah hung it out."

"A little odd, isn't it? I mean, the pool has been dry since yesterday morning, so she can't have been swimming." The schoolteacher looked at the brief lastex garment, made so form-fitting that it had to be laced like a football at either side, and noticed that the laces had been tied tight and then torn instead of being untied.

"Helen never takes any care of her things," Lawn informed her. "I used to have to mend them for her, and now Beulah has to do it."

They came into the kitchen, where Beulah, her face darker than usual, was cleaning up the table on which Searles had left the makings of his sandwich. She was mumbling something about "trash" but looked up blankly at Miss Withers's opening question.

"Yassum," she said. "I hanged out Miss' Cairns's suit. It sho' woulda mildewed fast, tucked down into her laundry bag all wet like she left it."

"When," asked Miss Withers softly, turning to Lawn, "just when was the last time your sister wore that suit that you know of?"

Lawn shrugged. "I don't know. She may have tried the pool out Friday, the day before the party. They'd filled it then."

"I see. I thought for a moment ..." Miss Withers shook her head. "By the way, I wonder how long it would take a man to remove his coat and shirt and then whisk them on again after he had done—well, whatever it was."

Lawn's eyes narrowed. "Still aiming at Pat? A man, I know, has lots of buttons on his shirt, and then there's a necktie and all that. Of course Searles doesn't wear a tie, but he wears a sweater under that foul old jacket, and probably long underwear under that. But—but a woman! It would be easy enough for a woman, because women usually wear loose sleeves that could roll to the shoulder in a jiffy——"

"You mean, darling, sleeves like the ones on the dress I wore at the party?" They both looked up with a start to see Helen, a symphony in black, standing in the door of the dining room. Behind her was Thurlow Abbott, looking older and tireder.

The two sisters faced each other, and for a moment Miss Withers could see a resemblance between them, which flickered and was gone. "Why, yes," Lawn said slowly. "Helen, I want to talk to you."

"Surely not now!" Helen said. "It wouldn't be any use. You see, I know what you're up to. You've failed to pin this mess on to Pat, and so you've decided on me."

There was a long silence. "You're so beautiful," Lawn told her. "And so good. It's a shame that you couldn't have been just a little brighter!" The girl turned towards Miss Withers. "Please excuse me, it's getting very, very stuffy in here. I'm going to change my clothes and then go down and have a long talk with the horses in Mame Boad's stable." She ran out of the room.

"My daughter Lawn," said Thurlow Abbott in his croaking voice, "gets more difficult every day. By the way, Miss Withers, may I ask just what it was you wanted?"

"To find out how and why your son-in-law was murdered, and who did it!"

"But it wasn't murder!" Helen cut in. "Didn't you know? The police are being awfully slow and stupid about it all, but I thought you would see. When they drained the pool yesterday they found Huntley's wrist-watch at the bottom. He must have missed it when he was dressing after his swim and rushed out just as he was. In trying to reach it, he fell in and was drowned."

"Huntley was, I'm afraid, a very week swimmer," Thurlow Abbott chimed in. "Not the athletic type at all, you know."

"And that watch was his pride and joy," Helen added. "Huntley loved gadgety things like that. He'd have gone almost out of his mind if he'd looked at his wrist and seen that it was missing."

"Was he so proud of it," Miss Withers probed gently, "that he'd have gone swimming without noticing that he'd left it on?"

Helen thought he might. "You see, except in the tub, he never took it off, not even when he slept. It was waterproof and shockproof and everything proof."

The schoolteacher stilled an impulse to ask if the watch had been equipped with an outboard motor too—so that it could travel from the shallow end of the pool, where a poor swimmer like Cairns would presumably have been disporting himself, down to the deep end, fifty feet or more away. But for the moment that could wait. She smiled at Helen Cairns and then asked, "There is just one other thing I must ask you now. Where did your late husband hide things?"

The beautiful face went blank. "Hide things? But he didn't. He wasn't the hiding type. Why, he even told me what I was getting for my birthdays and Christmases weeks before the day."

"I wasn't thinking of presents," Miss Withers went on. "I was wondering whatever became of the book—the book with the red jacket. *Oriental Moments* was the title, I believe."

She had great hopes of that shot in the dark, but it fizzled out like a wet firecracker. Either Helen and her father had never heard of the book, or else they were far better actors than she had given them credit for. And long experience with the little hellions of her third-grade classes back at Jefferson School had taught her a number of ways to tell when any one is lying. She shrugged. "Well, perhaps it will turn up when we least expect it. Like your white bathing suit."

Helen froze. "My what?"

"Your white bathing suit that your maid found in your laundry bag in grave danger of mildew."

"I don't understand." Helen was frowning, but she looked a little pale. "I used the suit Friday, but—I'm sure I left it in the dressing room."

"Did you really? Well, thank you very much, anyway. I'm on my way down to the jail now, in hopes of seeing the proper authorities and getting young Montague released. He couldn't have drowned your husband, Mrs. Cairns. The rake wasn't long enough. Would you have any message for Pat, in case I get in to see him?"

Helen looked quickly at her father, who still hovered nervously in the background. "Why, no. Of course not." But she walked with Miss Withers through the house, almost to the front door. Making sure that they were alone, she produced from her breast a thin packet of letters tied neatly with red string. "Just give these back to him, will you, before the

police find them. Tell him—oh, there's nothing I can say to Pat now!"
Helen turned and went back towards the stairs, half-running, and with a
handkerchief pressed to her mouth.

Miss Withers stood stock-still, looking after her. Then she saw Thurlow Abbott coming towards her, his face strained and drawn. "I hope
you'll make allowances for my daughter Helen," he said. "She is very
distrait. An old, forgotten love popping up suddenly out of the past, re-
viving old memories—"

"Forgotten?" Miss Withers echoed doubtfully.

"Helen fancied herself in love with young Montague many years ago,"
Abbott told her. "It was nothing but a boy-and-girl affair, really. They
were not suited to each other in any way. I tried of course to advise her,
but it is difficult for a father to be a mother."

"I can imagine," agreed the schoolteacher.

"Er—yes. It was very lucky for everyone concerned that the draft took
the young man away."

"For everyone except the young man, at any rate."

Abbott didn't smile. "It was unfortunate that he returned. You see,
Helen is the sentimental feminine type. Not at all like Lawn."

Miss Withers could agree with him there, at any rate. "Your daughters
do seem rather unlike, for sisters," she angled hopefully.

"Half-sisters," he confessed in his sepulchral voice. "A minor poet
who once visited our house said that Helen and Lawn typified the women
of Eden. Eve and Lilith, you know. The wife and the mistress type."

"Very poetic," agreed Miss Withers. "But after all, it was Eve who got
into trouble with the snake, wasn't it? I never heard anything scandalous
about Lilith, outside of her being an Assyrian demon, of course."

Thurlow Abbott wasn't listening; he was merely waiting for her to
stop talking so that he could start again. "I do wish, Miss Withers," he
said, coming closer, "that you would take anything Lawn says to you
with a big grain of salt. You see, Helen's mother was a choir singer, a very
sweet and gentle person. After her tragic death—she was the first woman
to be killed in a motor car accident on Long Island—I traveled for a few
seasons, and there in vaude—I mean, in concert, I fell in with a very
fascinating wildcat of a woman. The Princess Zoraida, Egyptian mystic,
she called herself. Her powers were, to tell the truth, unusual. She was
Lawn's mother."

"Really! And she abandoned you with the babe in your arms? It sounds
a little like *Way Down East* in reverse."

"It was on Pan-time, in Seattle," Abbott corrected her. "Of course the

Princess and I had gone through a ceremony, but I had reason after she walked out on me to think that she already had a husband or two scattered throughout the theatrical profession."

"How very unfortunate. It cannot be easy for a man to try to bring up two children."

He bowed. "I had hoped, of course, that they would carry on the Abbott name in the theater, but it was not to be. Helen has the beauty but not the temperament. And Lawn—I'm afraid that the consciousness of her dark heritage has embittered her. She has never felt that she belonged, in spite of everything that I could do." Thurlow Abbott sighed heavily. "You understand, of course."

"I think I'm beginning to," admitted Miss Withers, and took her departure.

CHAPTER NINE

Having taken her departure, Miss Hildegarde Withers had to bring it back, ring the Cairns bell, and politely request permission to use the telephone in order to summon a taxi. As it turned out, she might as well have saved her breath, for the hotel desk informed her that both the local vehicles were out on calls.

There was nothing for it, then, but to march out upon the highway and head towards town. The schoolteacher had barely got into her stride when a small black coupé came rocking along behind her. She hastily made the universal gesture with her thumb, and the car slowed down.

It turned out to be Mame Boad at the wheel, headed for town to do her marketing and obviously pleased at having company. She was considerably less happy a few minutes later when Miss Withers reminded her of their previous meeting.

"I have been thinking a good deal lately," the schoolteacher said, "about the call that you and Dr. Radebaugh and Commander Bennington paid upon me when I first came to Shoreham."

"Oh, that!" answered Mrs. Boad. "Nothing of importance, really. We were all upset at the time, of course. But since then the situation has changed."

"You mean, otherwise taken care of?" Miss Withers pressed wickedly.

Mame Boad did not answer, but twin spots of orange rouge flamed suddenly on her cheekbones. They rode on in silence for perhaps half a mile. "I've been thinking of dropping in on you for a chat one of these days," Miss Withers continued. "You're the Cairnses' nearest neighbor, are you not?"

Mrs. Boad thought about it and then cautiously admitted that she guessed she was. "Huntley Cairns bought the place last year, and they lived in the old house until they started to tear it down to make room for the new one."

"And Mrs. Cairns's sister uses your stable?"

"We keep her horse, yes. Of course Cairns pays—or paid—half the wages of the groom who comes in by the day."

"A very cooperative arrangement. I suppose that a wild, violent girl like Lawn is pretty hard on horseflesh, isn't she?"

"What?" The little car jerked slightly. "Lord, no! That girl takes her big gelding out every day, and half the time instead of giving him a decent workout she'll get off and let him graze, or just trot him along in the surf to strengthen his forelegs. Willy—that's the groom—says that Lawn has never once brought that fellow in sweating. She likes to do most of the grooming, too, fixes him bran mashes and all that sort of thing. I think she likes horses better than people."

"A point of view not too unreasonable, in view of the sort of world we live in. By the way, Mrs. Boad, curiosity has always been my besetting sin. I wonder if you'd tell me just what it was that you and your friends were so anxious to have me investigate some weeks ago. It needn't go any further—"

Mame Boad sailed serenely through a boulevard stop. "But I'm afraid I can't answer that question," she said abruptly. "At least not now. Perhaps after I have the consent of the others involved … The matter was personal and very delicate, you see."

"More delicate than murder? I wonder." Miss Withers received no answer to that and had expected none. "By the way, if you are going in that direction, please drop me off at the police station. Or on second thought, right here on the corner. I believe there's a bookstore—yes, there it is. Thank you so much."

Even after she was inside the shop Miss Withers could see Mame Boad peering in at her from the black coupé as she drove slowly away. "Let her stew a little," decided the schoolteacher calmly. A clerk approached her, and she asked for a copy of *Oriental Moments*.

The young man tugged at his wisp of moustache for a moment and then gave it as his opinion that she wouldn't be able to buy a copy in Shoreham. "It came out last year, I believe, but there wasn't much call for it," he told her. "It's probably out of print now, but we could try ordering it for you."

She shook her head slowly. The young man came closer and lowered his voice. "We do happen to have a copy of *The Chinese Room*, and *Trio*, and—"

"I beg your pardon!" Miss Withers shook her head emphatically. "Is *Oriental Moments* that sort of book?"

He smiled. "No, madam. But from the title, certain of our customers have thought so."

She turned and headed out of the store, but in the doorway she heard him add: "I think there's a copy in the rental library downstairs, if it isn't out."

There was, and it wasn't. A moment later, at the price of library membership and upon her promise to pay three cents a day for its use, Miss Hildegarde Withers came into temporary possession of *Oriental Moments*, red jacket and all. Moreover, on a card stuck into the front of the book was a list of the names of previous renters. This she studied with great care, but the only one implicated in the Cairns case who was listed there turned out to be Adele Beale, and that had been more than six months ago.

The schoolteacher went out into the street with her nose buried in the volume, expecting the worst, in spite of what the clerk had said, because of the provocative Chinese damsel depicted undressed on the cover. But the book turned out to be a series of notes and impressions of life in Chungking by a State Department employee stranded there during the time it was the temporary wartime capital.

From the first few pages Miss Withers could see that the author, in typical State Department fashion, had been bored with his work, superior to the Chinese, jittery about the Russians, and consistently myopic about the actual forces and cross-purposes which had been surging all around him. There were pages and pages about receptions and cocktail parties, with detailed accounts of the extreme difficulty of getting Scotch flown in over the Hump from India, but what this had to do with the murder of Huntley Cairns, or anything else, Miss Withers was at the moment unable to tell.

She came down the street, still reading, and very nearly turned into the Elite Turkish Baths for Gentlemen Only instead of her proper destination. Crossing the street, she was about to enter the Shoreham police station when she heard a shrill whistle behind her and turned to face Lawn Abbott. The girl was wearing, in addition to open shirt, blue jeans, and jodhpur shoes, a very worried expression.

"Fancy meeting you here!" said Miss Withers.

"Wait, oh, please wait," Lawn cried, "before you go in. Are you going to try to get permission to see Pat?"

"Among other things, yes."

"I have to talk to you first. It's very important."

Miss Withers smiled and nodded. "Important to whom?"

"To—to Pat, of course. Listen, did my sister give you some old letters to return to him?"

"Some *what*?"

"Oh, don't be like that at a time like this. I know she did. It would be just like her. I know where she kept them hidden, and they weren't there, so I charged her with it. She denied it, but Helen can't fool me. That's why I rushed down here. You mustn't return those to Pat!"

"And why not, child?"

"Read them," Lawn said bitterly. "I have. I suppose you wouldn't consider it strictly honorable, but I found them in an old cookbook, where she had them cached. Nobody ever looks into a cookbook, not in our house anyway. Don't you see what I'm driving at? Those letters were mostly written to Helen after she was married. Pat was overseas and very bitter. He said a lot of things about Huntley and what he'd like to do to him, things that the police could twist—"

"But your sister didn't say anything about my giving them to the police!"

"She thought perhaps you would, though. You're supposed to be such friends with that inspector from New York. Or maybe she asked you to slip them to Pat in jail—where ten to one they'd be discovered and taken away from him. I have my own ideas about why Helen did it. It couldn't be that she was just trying to get rid of the letters or she could have burned them."

"At any rate," Miss Withers decided firmly, "the letters can stay right where they are for the time being." She patted her capacious pocketbook firmly. "At the moment I'm much more interested in something else. Have you ever seen this book before?"

Lawn stared blankly at *Oriental Moments*. Then she shook her head. "But why—"

"I don't quite know why," Miss Withers began, and broke off as the door beside them opened and Jed Nicolet came out, hurrying a little. He seemed about to plunge past them when Lawn turned and called. Surprised, he turned, recognized Lawn, and his sharp, vulpine face brightened.

"Hello-ello!" he said. "What's up? Are you two hunting together now?"

"I was about to make an effort to see the prisoner," Miss Withers admitted. "How is he taking it?"

The lawyer shrugged. "How should I know?"

"But I thought an attorney could always get in to see his client."

"He is supposed to, according to the law. If he can find where said client is being held. I could even have had him out on a writ, I think, only—"

"Only the police have him hidden somewhere?" Miss Withers nodded slowly. The inspector was up to his old tricks.

"Nothing like that," Jed Nicolet admitted. "Pat is upstairs all right, in one of the nice moldy cells that the county provides. Only it seems that he has decided that he doesn't want a lawyer, and if he does have a lawyer he doesn't want me." Nicolet started to laugh a little nervously. Then he stopped laughing and choked.

"What's the matter?" Lawn demanded.

"Nothing—nothing at all," Nicolet said. His face, Miss Withers noticed, was gray. "See you later," he called over his shoulder, and went hurrying down to the sidewalk.

"Whatever in the world!" gasped Miss Withers.

"Jed isn't himself at all," Lawn murmured softly. "Do you suppose— he seemed to be staring at that book in your hand."

"I noticed that too."

"But why should he turn white and run off as if somebody were after him?"

"It is just remotely possible," observed the schoolteacher, "that somebody is!"

Lawn thought about that remark for a long moment. "I think I see what you mean," the girl said. "That would change everything, wouldn't it? I mean, if the triangle idea was all wrong and the police had to start looking—"

"For a hexagon? In my opinion this entire case is much more complicated than any figure in plane geometry. It's trigonometry, at least. Well, I came down here to make an attempt to see Pat Montague. Do you want to come with me?"

Lawn hesitated. "I can't bear to think of Pat behind bars. I can't bear to think of anybody behind bars, for that matter. It isn't humane to lock people up. I've been there myself, you see."

"You have?"

"Oh, didn't you know? Yes, I spent three days locked up when I was seventeen." She laughed suddenly at Miss Withers's expression. "Oh, it wasn't anything so very criminal. It was just that I'd run away from home, and the Atlanta police held me until father could come down and lead me home in disgrace."

"You've had quite a career, haven't you?" Miss Withers's voice was faintly envious.

"An unlucky one, at least so far," Lawn admitted. "And right now I don't think I'd have much luck with Pat Montague. Not that I wouldn't like to …" She shook her head. "I guess I'll run along."

"Shall I give him a message?"

"Why …" Lawn thought. "Just tell him that I know he's innocent and that it won't be long before everybody else knows it too." She pressed Miss Withers's arm and turned back swiftly towards the curb and Helen's light car, which she had parked there at an angle. "I'd better get this heap home before my sister gets more furious at me than she is already. Good night, and good luck."

Miss Withers stared after her. "It's the younger generation, knock-knock-knocking at the door," she hummed to herself. She was suddenly glad that she had never tried bringing up anything more complicated than kittens, puppies, canaries, and tropical fish.

She went on inside the station, found an elderly man in uniform picking his teeth at the desk, and asked in her politest tone for an audience with the prisoner.

"Can't see him!" pronounced that guardian of law and order. He nodded towards the stairs. "The sheriff and that New York cop are up there with him now."

"It's that New York cop that I really want to see," Miss Withers advised him, and headed up the stair before he could answer. She had some trouble with a big barred-iron gate at the head of the stair, but finally she hammered upon it until she had drawn the irate attention of the turnkey, Sheriff Vinge, and the inspector.

"Let her in," said Piper wearily. "And it's okay with me if you keep her in. What is it now, Hildegarde?"

"I want five minutes with the prisoner, whether he likes it or not, and I think he'll not."

"How about it, Sheriff?" the inspector asked, introducing them.

"Well, now, since this's the lady that turned him in—" Sheriff Vinge was anxious to be friendly. "Oh, go ahead, ma'am. Last cell on the right, and we'll be watching, so don't try to slip him any hacksaws or skeleton keys."

"I don't want to slip Pat Montague anything but a piece of my mind," said Miss Withers, and hurried on. She found Montague sitting on his cot, looking rather confused and irritable, which, she supposed, was only to be expected.

"How do you do, young man?" she greeted him.

Pat Montague looked up at her, blinked, and said, "Oh, God!"

"I know how you feel," she went on hastily, peering through the bars. "I admit that I gravely misjudged you the other night, but since that time I've done my best to rectify the error, really, I have."

Montague stood up and came towards her. "Forget it. I was sore at the world, but this is a good place to cool off and think things over. Besides, it was all Nicolet's fault. He should have minded his own business in the first place."

"Perhaps he was. But never mind that. I have a message for you." She waited a moment, but there was only a slight flicker of interest. "Aren't you going to ask if it's from Helen?"

His face was clouded. "All right, is it?"

"As a matter of fact, no. From her sister. Lawn said to tell you that she knows you're innocent and that pretty soon everyone else will know it too."

A faint but engaging smile lighted his face, and Miss Withers understood why women were so intrigued with Pat Montague. "Thanks," he said. "She's a good kid, I guess, after all. She's changed a lot since I went away."

"Everything changes in three years. You've changed. And so, for that matter, has Helen."

Pat winced slightly under that jab. "I wouldn't know," he said hopelessly. "For a long time I thought that if I could only see her, just once—"

"But didn't you? I mean, for just a second, when you looked down from the roadway to the swimming pool that afternoon?"

"But that wasn't Helen!" he said quickly. "It couldn't have been. She was just so much in my mind that I thought anyone in a white bathing suit was her. It must have been Cairns I saw. There was time for it to happen while I was walking down from the road—it's about a quarter of a mile, you know."

"Still a very neat, carefully timed job of murder," she said.

He wasn't listening. "Miss Withers, will you be seeing Helen again soon?"

"Perhaps. Why?"

"Just tell her that as soon as I get out of here I'm going as far away as I can get, as fast as I can. Maybe I'll reenlist; I worked my way up once and I can do it again. I don't think I'd like being a civilian very much, anyway. I came back expecting things to be the same, and they seem all changed and different—"

"To you and ten million other young men," said Miss Withers.

"Tell her I'm sorry I tried to come barging back into things, and she may as well forget me."

"That," pointed out the schoolteacher, "is a rather delicate message to carry."

"You mean it will hurt her?"

"It will hurt somebody," Miss Withers hinted. This was most certainly not, she realized, the opportune time to hand him the packet of love letters, even if she had intended to, which she hadn't.

"I must run along," she said. "There is just one question. When Searles came up to you at the pool just a moment after you discovered the body, how was he dressed?"

"Dressed? In overalls, I guess. I can't remember."

"Of course you can remember. Didn't he have his coat over his arm and his sleeves rolled up?"

Pat shut his eyes hard, scowling. "No, he didn't! He was wearing his jacket—a dirty old denim jacket."

"But the sleeves—were they soaked?"

Pat saw what she was driving at and shook his head. "They were dry," he admitted. "I wish I could say they were wet, but they weren't, not then, anyway."

And that, as Miss Withers said later to the inspector, was that. She found Piper waiting for her at the gate of the lockup and went downstairs with him. "But what are you so glum about, Oscar? Having trouble getting evidence enough on Pat Montague to take to the grand jury?"

"There might be a snag or two in that quarter," he admitted.

"Such as the length of the murder weapon, so called?"

He grinned. "I figured you'd get on to the rake handle sooner or later. Yes, that among other things. You know what we were talking about to Pat Montague when you came busting in? He wants to be put to the lie-detector test. You know what I think of those machines, anyway. It's possible to beat them if you know enough about how they work and have pretty good control of yourself. That's especially true when the test isn't given by an expert, and the sheriff is a little dubious about okaying the expense of sending out to Evanston for one of Keeler's bright young men."

"But it speaks well for the prisoner, doesn't it? I mean his requesting the machine."

"A smart lawyer could certainly make it look that way, yes. Or if the newspapers got hold of the request, which they haven't yet. And don't you go talking!"

"Perish the thought!" Miss Withers was about to say more, but at that moment the officer at the desk beckoned to the inspector, holding up the phone.

"It's for you, sir!"

Piper picked it up, said, "Speaking," and listened for some time. Then he said, "Thanks, Georgie," and hung up. He came back to Miss Withers, grinning from ear to ear.

"Well?" she demanded. "Come clean!"

He hesitated. "I don't know what it means, probably nothing—but it's a sidelight on Cairns. That was what you wanted, wasn't it? You know how the guy made all his money?"

"Public relations, somebody said."

"That means nowadays almost anything you want it to mean. But Huntley Cairns was no fool. He stumbled on to a gold mine of an idea and parleyed it into a fortune. His firm was really a super deluxe machine for swamping motion-picture studios, radio chains, and stage producers with letters. After we had our talk this morning I got the man who'd done the original investigation to go back to Cairns Associates and get tough, and he uncovered the whole thing."

"Letters!" she echoed. "But why?"

"Those people are all supersensitive to what they call the public pulse. About the only way they can gauge public demand is by the fan mail they get. They never actually read it, but they have it tabulated and all that sort of thing. For instance, let's suppose that Joey Jones is a radio comedian and he wants his sponsor to renew his contract. He simply comes to Cairns Associates and hires them to start up the machine. They have a couple of hundred letter-writers, mostly women who work at home. They're supplied with all the various kinds of pens and inks and pencils and typewriters of all makes and sizes and type styles. All sorts of notepaper, too. The letters are collected centrally and then distributed for mailing at post offices in the towns where the client especially wants to show he has a devoted following. A few days later the sponsor begins to get thousands of letters, all screaming that they will never buy any more of his underarm deodorant unless they can hear Joey Jones every Thursday night. Or unless Dawn O'Day gets to play the lead in A-budget pictures, or unless Marmaduke Glutz plays *Hamlet* on Broadway this year."

"But, Oscar, is it legal?"

"Perfectly. They used phone books and city directories to get the names and addresses in case of a checkup or a form-letter answer, but they changed the names or initials just a little, enough to keep clear of forgery charges. Cairns got from ten to twenty-five cents a letter, depending on what the traffic would bear. For a thousand dollars anybody could get up to ten thousand letters, which would be less than one week's salary and deductible from the income tax as a legitimate expense, anyway."

Miss Withers thought about it. "Very clever of Cairns. It does sound like a gold mine."

"It is—or was. And just think of the unfunny comics, the matronly ingenues, the gravel-voiced tenors who have been shoved down the public's throat because Cairns Associates made the big-money advertisers, the theatrical and movie producers, think that the public couldn't get along without them!"

"Oscar, could the murder motive have come out of that?"

He was amused. "I don't think the National Association of Manufacturers drowned Cairns. And the long-suffering public can't very well protect itself, or we'd have had an end of crooners and double-talk comics and soap operas years ago."

"How about a dissatisfied client?"

The inspector shook his head. "The clients weren't dissatisfied. The Cairns system even now and then gave an unknown a chance. Those Linton twins who were at the cocktail party had signed up with Cairns, and he was all set to put on a letter campaign to get them the movie role in *Forever Amber*—you know, as a novelty. One actress has played a dual role, why not two actresses playing one? Cairns was charging them a double rate because they were unknowns, but that's no motive for them to bump him off. We're keeping an eye on them, though, because we don't want to miss angles."

"Or any curves, you mean? Gracious, Oscar, and at your age too!"

"Aw—" The inspector grinned and waved his hand. "You run along, I've got to get back to work. The commissioner will be wondering why I take so long to wind a case like this up and put it away."

"In my private opinion," the schoolteacher said, "this case is going to wind itself up, and right speedily too."

He stared at her. "You haven't been throwing monkey wrenches around in the machinery, have you?"

"Not intentionally. But in my helpful way I just possibly have been acting as a sort of catalytic agent. I feel it in my bones that something is going to happen, maybe tonight."

"You and your hunches! Be a good girl and get back to your tropical fish and let me worry about clues, will you?"

She paused in the doorway. "Yes, Oscar, but suppose you haven't considered the right clues! I mean the Book with the Red Jacket, and the Returned Letters, and the Mildewed Bathing Suit, and—"

"Save it," he said. "I'll be over later, and you can riddle me your riddles then. And if Pat Montague comes through with a confession in the meantime, you'll be the first to know."

"I'm glad," Miss Hildegarde Withers called after him, "that I don't have to sit on a hot stove until *that* happens!"

CHAPTER TEN

Once safe at home, the schoolteacher went directly to her aquarium, as a clairvoyant to her crystal ball or a gypsy to her tea leaves. Through pale jade water the jeweled fish still moved in their pathless ways. After she had stared at them close up for a little while Miss Withers felt herself once more losing her identity, moving through the glass exactly like Alice. Yet this was a stranger world than Wonderland or the regions that bordered on Looking-Glass House.

It was a world of sudden changes. Overnight one of the bright Paris-green plants, a sturdy spatterdock, had shot up one sprout several inches, reaching almost to the surface of the water. A fat mystery snail climbed, as she watched, up to the top of the marine world and then stretched out a trunk-like arm to suck in air. After a moment he let go his hold, bubble and all, and floated dreamily down to the bottom to start all over again. "Very much the way I've been carrying on," Miss Withers decided.

A long, snaky dojo slid along the bottom of the tank, sucking in sand and spitting it out again, and then suddenly gave up its scavenging and swam sinuously up to a crotch in one of the feathery *allisneria* plants, where it coiled itself up for all the world like a boa constrictor in a jungle tree.

And ever and always the jeweled fish moved in their everlasting journey to nowhere. All except one of the rosy tetras, who now floated belly-up against the farther side of the tank, behind the thermostat. As the schoolteacher, shocked and horrified, retrieved the tiny corpse with the aid of a dip net, she saw that the tail fin had been bitten clean away.

Down in the lower corner of the tank the female *betta* followed her mate as always, goggle eyes admiring his peacock perfection. In the jade distance behind the pile of rocks the two angelfish floated serenely, their long antennae sweeping back, their mouths moving in what seemed to be a silent whisper. One of them, however, had a slight list to starboard.

"I'd like to be a mermaid for about five minutes," Miss Withers said grimly. "I'd get to the bottom of this business."

But since that metamorphosis seemed out of the question, the school ma'am sat down and tried to find out something closer to the realms of possibility. "I'm a fine one," she told herself, "to attempt the unraveling of a murder mystery when I can't even fathom this epidemic of cannibalism in my own aquarium."

Somehow, in spite of all reason, a strange sort of parallel was taking shape—between the midget murders among her tropical fish and the greater problem which had disrupted the placid little town of Shoreham. She had a completely unreasonable feeling that if she solved one she would solve the other too.

Which reminded her that she was rather behind on her reading. *Oriental Moments* came first on the list, and it was not until she was well into the fifth chapter that she found anything at all which could possibly have any bearing on the matter at hand. Here, however, she paused, reread the paragraph, and turned down a corner of the page. She put the little book back into her handbag with a nod of satisfaction.

Then she took up the packet of letters written to Helen by Pat Montague and untied the string. Then she stopped for a moment. "I do hope," said Miss Withers to herself, "that I am doing this out of pure scientific necessity and not just being a meddlesome old maid. It is certainly an invasion of privacy, and yet Huntley Cairns had his privacy invaded when his life was choked out of him."

The police, even the inspector, would read them like a shot and probably hand them over to the newspapers later; she knew that much.

Finally, after a considerable debate with her New England conscience, she decided, as she had known all along that she would, to read the letters. After five minutes she decided that Helen should never have kept them and after ten minutes she decided that Pat Montague should never have written them.

The first was dated the day before D-Day, presumably from somewhere in England, and the rest had been written at various times across France and Belgium, and the final one somewhere east of the Rhine.

They were love letters, strong, passionate love letters, and yet obviously letters written by a man who had not expected to live through the hell on Omaha Beach, the seesaw in Normandy, the Battle of the Bulge, and the final assault on the Rhine and the Fortress Europa. His very fatalism had made Pat Montague write as he would never and could never have written otherwise—certainly not to another man's wife.

They were strange, bitter letters, saying much but leaving more unsaid. Huntley Cairns was mentioned only once, and that when Pat wrote that early that morning he had mowed down three German engineers with a B.A.R., and that it had helped him to kill them to think that they were Cairns, each of them.

"Oh, dear!" murmured Miss Withers. "What Oscar Piper—and the sheriff—could make of that!"

She tied up the letters very carefully and put them back into her handbag.

It seemed the safest place, next to the fire—and if they were to be destroyed, Pat Montague would have to do the destroying.

Anyway, there were more immediate problems. She looked up an address in the classified section of the telephone book and then put on a hat which resembled an unkempt window-box, took up her umbrella, and set forth into the thick, muggy afternoon.

She walked halfway across the town and turned into the doorway of a small, neatly whitewashed building which bore a large sign, "Small Pet Hospital," and beneath that, "D. M. Harvey, Veterinary Surgeon."

Dr. Harvey turned out to be a thin, youngish man with sandy hair brushed so tightly back from his forehead that it seemed to pull his eyebrows up half an inch. He smelled of disinfectant and of dog. His eyebrows went up another notch when she told him what had brought her here.

"Well, aren't tropical fish small pets?" she demanded.

The vet laughed. "I guess you got me there, all right. But I'm sorry to say that I haven't had much practice with fish, except for a few trout that I manage to kill when I get away over to Jersey and find a nice handy little stream. Most of my business is clipping and defleaing cats and dogs, and half of that went blooie when they put out the new DDT sprays for animals."

Miss Withers was properly sympathetic. "But didn't they teach you anything about fish when you studied veterinary medicine?"

"Not much, I'm afraid." Then he brightened. "But I've got a lot of reference books. Some of them might help us. Wait a minute."

Dr. Harvey left her and returned after a few minutes with a heavy tome.

"There seems to be one chapter in Malden and Larrier that applies. Let's see—here we are. 'Fungus Diseases in the Small Aquarium. Parasites, Microscopic and Larger. Hazards of the Community Tank'—this is it." His thick chemical-stained finger marked a page.

Miss Withers read: "'Not all tropical fishes can be successfully kept in a community tank, for it must be remembered that all fish are naturally cannibalistic. In most cases, however, the whole problem can be resolved to a matter of size, as fish do not ordinarily prey upon other fish, of whatever species, who are of approximately half their own bulk or more. However, even among the same species, fish will without hesitation eat or attempt to eat any other fish of less than half their size, even in most cases including their own young. Most tropical fish remain in their desired miniature size in an aquarium, one exception to this being the *scalare* or angelfish, which grow even under those conditions and which should be removed from the tank as soon as they reach the size of a half-dollar.' "

She sniffed. "That doesn't apply—my angelfish are only the size of quarters." She read on: "'Two male *bettas*, or Siamese fighting fish, will of course battle to the death if kept in the same tank, and the female *betta* has an unsavory reputation for attacking other females, and sometimes any other fish, probably out of pure jealousy. Likewise the red-bellied dace and the black-banded miniature sunfish have been known to transgress. It must further be remembered that any tropical fish other than the scavengers or soft-mouthed varieties may become a killer in a community tank, just as some dogs learn to kill sheep, and having once acquired the habit will continue until caught and eliminated. Only trial and error will assist the fish fancier in this matter.' "

She closed the book. "It seems to boil down to this—that all fish, like mankind, were murderers in the wild state and have a tendency to revert." Miss Withers consulted the gold watch which was pinned to her bosom.

"Dear me, I had no idea that I had stayed so long. Forgive me, Doctor, I know you must have more important problems than mine."

He accepted a two-dollar fee with modest reluctance. "Oh, we're not so busy now," said Dr. Harvey pleasantly.

"Not as busy as you were some months ago, then?"

He blinked. "Oh, you know about that? I thought it had been pretty well hushed up—bad for the summer visitor trade, you know, and half Shoreham lives on that. People don't want to come out here and have their pets curl up and die."

"Naturally not."

"Once a dog-poisoning epidemic starts, it's hard to stop it. We lost forty-six dogs here in Shoreham, a pretty good percentage of the canine population."

"As many as that? I suppose, Doctor, that you performed autopsies on the poisoned animals? What was it, the usual strychnine?"

He shook his head. "Arsenic, at first. Then carbon tetrachloride and pyridine. And finally, three or four of the dogs that I examined showed no trace of poison at all. The cause of death was really peritonitis—simple perforation of the peritoneum—"

"By a sliver of bamboo?"

Dr. Harvey backed away from her very quickly indeed. "Now, how did you find that out?" he demanded. "Either somebody has been talking that had no business to talk, or else—"

"Oh, I get around," Miss Withers told him, and hastily got out of the place.

She went hurrying back down the street, feeling at the moment some of the confusion of a hound puppy let loose on a wood lot where the overlaid scents of rabbit, squirrel, partridge, and red fox crisscrossed everywhere. She had to take herself firmly in hand in order to resist a tendency to give tongue and blindly rush off in all directions at once.

The particular avenue which opened up in front of her might be, she realized all too well, only a blind alley. But it was one of the smoothest, straightest alleys, and downhill all the way. Besides, it was better to be doing something than to be doing nothing.

"Now's the time," Miss Withers said to herself, "to send a monkey to pull the chestnuts out of the fire." Or was it the cat who burned its paws in the fabled operation? She had never got it quite straight. At any rate, she needed help in baiting a certain harmless little trap that she had worked out in her mind.

She thought of several possibilities, discarding them almost at once. Then she looked again at the little red volume in her handbag and nodded slowly. A block or so along the street she saw one of the local taxicabs cruising slowly towards her, and on an impulse she hailed it and demanded to be hauled to the Beale residence.

"Anywhere you say, lady," said the driver. "Say, tell me something. Ain't you the she-Hawkshaw from New York that's supposed to be trying to figure out what happened to Huntley Cairns?"

Miss Withers realized that there was no keeping of secrets in a town this size and reluctantly admitted her interest in the affair. "I don't suppose that you have a theory about the case?" she asked.

"Inside job," he came back promptly.

"I had considered that angle myself," she admitted. "And so, I imagine, have the police."

"Don't kid yourself the police will get anywhere with a tough one like this Cairns job," he told her. "They're handing out stuff to the papers about how they have a hot clue and an arrest is expected any minute. That's a lot of bilge. Before I was in the service I might a fell for it, but not now. I seen too many official training films and read too many of Doug's communiques."

Miss Withers blinked and agreed that military service did alter the viewpoint and the gullibility of many young men. She wondered, as she rode along, just how much Pat Montague had altered. Perhaps the changes were deep within him and he was not entirely aware of them as yet.

Otherwise why would he remain a nympholept, in love with a romantic dream girl who couldn't ever have existed? He might not be in love with Helen at all—not the living, breathing girl. Maybe he was even falling in love with somebody else without knowing it yet.

When they pulled up in front of the Beale residence she saw that no car was in the driveway, which meant that Midge Beale was still at work and that she could have a heart-to-heart talk with Adele. Asking the driver to wait, she marched stiffly up the steps to ring the bell. But even as her thumb hovered on the button Miss Withers caught her breath sharply. She saw two or three dull brownish stains on the cement step—pear-shaped spots, surrounded by satellites.

Automatically the schoolteacher reached down to touch one and then studied the smear on the tip of her glove. "'Will all great Neptune's ocean wash *this*?' " she murmured. For this was blood, there couldn't be the slightest doubt in the world about that.

The door, she noticed now, was not completely closed. She pushed at it very gently, and it swung inward. The little foyer and the living room behind it were empty and still. In spite of the heat of the thick, muggy afternoon the windows were all closed. She took one step inside, and then another. She sniffed and decided that the place smelled of stale tobacco and ashes in the trays, of gin and lemon peel and dust.

Miss Withers took another step and saw a dark spot the size of a dime on the sand-colored broadloom carpet ahead of her—and another one beyond that. The trail led in the direction of the stairs, a line of blood-stains a foot or so apart.

On she went—on, and up the steps. She hesitated once, when the first step creaked under her foot, but the taxicab waiting outside gave her some moral support, at any rate. Curiosity overruled prudence, and besides, the house was absolutely still. She tiptoed up the stairs.

The carpet in the upper hall was of a darker, mulberry color, which made the trail much harder to follow. And the distance between the drops was greater. "Whoever left these stains," Miss Withers decided, "was moving or being carried up the stairs and along the hall, because the stains are pear-shaped, with the larger end ahead."

She went on very slowly. Just then a mildly bewildered voice spoke up behind her. "What in hell goes on here?"

"Hush!" scolded Miss Withers. "I'm trying to follow …" She whirled around to see Midge Beale, who looked sleepy, disheveled, and unshaven, clutching a dressing-gown around his knobby little body and peering at her as though he wasn't quite sure that she was real. "If you must know, I'm following a trail of bloodstains, young man!" she told him ominously.

"I know where it leads to," Midge suggested helpfully.

"I have no doubt that you do!" she came back. "Mr. Beale, under circumstances like this, trespassing in somebody else's house is quite permissible. What have you done with your wife?"

"The trail," he repeated. "It leads to my nose."

"What?"

"I get nosebleeds whenever I get excited or angry, which is one of the reasons I got 4-F rating in the draft. My nose bled all over the place, as you're finding out."

"A likely story!" she shot back at him, moving at the same time in retreat towards the head of the stairs. But Midge followed her. "Stay where you are, young man!" she challenged, raising the umbrella. "Or I'll call for help!"

Midge stopped. "Women!" he said very bitterly. "I guess it is just asking too much to expect them to make any sense. But do you mind telling me what you're here for?"

"I came here to see your wife."

"Not in," he said.

"Really? Then I wonder if you would be kind enough to tell me where I could locate her. Could I telephone?"

The young man snorted. "I told her where to go, but I don't think they have telephone service there. Anyway, Adele grabbed the car keys and went leaping out of the door …" He stopped, grabbing futilely for a handkerchief in his dressing-gown pocket. "There it goes again!"

He plunged into the bathroom, holding his head over the sink. Miss Withers, peering in the door, was forced to admit that he really did have a nosebleed.

"Have you tried a wad of tissue paper under the upper lip?" she suggested helpfully.

"We had an awful fight," he said. "I suppose Adele is on her way to her mother's, way to hell and gone up in Yonkers. For all of me, she can stay there."

"It must have been a very bitter misunderstanding," Miss Withers suggested. "Have you tried putting cotton up your nostril? I found that when one of my pupils got a nosebleed—"

"Bitter! I popped her one."

"Dear, dear!" Miss Withers wrung out a washcloth in cold water and applied it to the back of his neck.

"Well, I didn't like being made a fool of! Ever since I married her I've been bragging about what a household manager Adele was—she only had a small allowance and yet the place was always full of good food and liquor and she used to have money left over almost every week. And then today I found out that she's been getting her money from another man— and a married man, to boot!"

"You should have booted him, then," Miss Withers suggested.

Midge Beale watched the thick red gore splash on to the porcelain. "Twenty-five dollars every week!" he continued. "From Fatso Cairns, of all people. And Adele tried to tell me that it was just a business arrangement, or a sort of royalty. But she couldn't show me a contract or anything. I wouldn't even have found out about it, only she asked me for money when she'd already had her household allowance this week. No wonder she was such a whiz at making both ends meet. It's clear enough that she had something on Cairns and was making him pay off. Maybe it was breach of promise when he dropped her to marry Helen."

"In that case," Miss Withers argued reasonably, "he would hardly have continued the payments after Adele married you. And the smallness of the sum, plus the weekly regularity, would seem to argue against the blackmail theory. I'm sure there must be some explanation. Why don't you have a nice quiet talk—"

"You can't have a nice quiet talk with a woman who always bursts into tears," Midge objected. "No, thanks, I don't need another cloth. It seems to have let up."

"Then I must be running along," the schoolteacher said, "before I say anything that will get your nose started again. There was just one question, however. At the Cairns cocktail party, after your little session in the library—"

"Don't ask me for details about the rest of the party," Midge begged.

"About that time it got very, very drunk out. That was Helen's fault, for stranding me with two martinis."

"I was only going to ask if you noticed the absence of anybody about that time—any of the people who had been in the library?"

He shook his head. "The Benningtons were playing bridge with Jed Nicolet and Mame Boad," he informed her. "Doc. Radebaugh and Trudy Boad cut in for one or two hands."

"Then any one of the five—I mean six, counting the dummy—could have been absent for a while without being noticed?"

"Without being noticed by me, anyway," Midge assured her.

Miss Withers headed for the stairs. "I hope you'll forgive me," she apologized when she was at the door. "I mean, for my thoughts. But a trail of bloodstains—"

Midge gasped. "I get it! You thought that—I mean, that Adele was—"

"Well, wouldn't anybody think that?"

He was laughing. "Why, ma'am, I wouldn't harm a hair of her head, even though I'd just love to wring her pretty neck. You understand?"

"I suppose so," agreed Miss Withers doubtfully. "Oh, I almost forgot. Have you ever seen this book before?" She waved *Oriental Moments* in front of him.

"Huh?" he brightened. "I don't know for sure—but it looks like the book that Nicolet made so much fuss over in Cairns's library. It's the right color, anyway."

"I thought it would be. Then you didn't see the same book when your wife took it out of the rental library down town some months ago?"

Midge looked blank. Then his face cleared. "Oh, that! Sure, I remember, especially the drawing on the cover. I kidded the life out of Adele. She picked up the book, thinking by the title and the naked girl on the cover that it was hot stuff, but it turned out to be too dull to read. Once you put it down you couldn't pick it up."

"Really! Your wife kept it out for more than a week, I happen to know."

"You may know that, but you don't know Adele. She never returned any book in less than a week, and some she never returned. That's the way she's made."

"Oh?" said the schoolteacher.

"Just a coincidence," Midge assured her.

"I suppose so," agreed Miss Withers thoughtfully, and made her adieus. She rode back to the hotel in a thoughtful silence. No matter which way she headed, she wound up against a stone wall. "My autobiography," she said to herself, "ought to be titled *My Life and Times in Blind Alleys*."

CHAPTER ELEVEN

The phone rang three times and then was answered by "Miz Cyains's res'dence," spoken in a soft, chocolate-syrupy voice. There was a brief pause, then a giggle, and Lawn Abbott dropped into her own voice. "Speaking," she said. "Oh, don't mind me, Miss Withers—I was only clowning. What's up? Did you get into—I mean, did you see him?"

"I did—"

"Oh—please wait just a sec while I get comfortable with a cigarette and everything." Lawn carried the telephone, its luxuriously overlength cord trailing out behind, over to a divan. She held a cigarette to a lighter built to resemble a flintlock pistol and then got comfortable, which to her consisted of lying on the back of her neck with her boot-clad legs in the air. "Now tell all!" she begged.

"Pat Montague seems to be taking his confinement as well as can be expected," the schoolteacher began. "It is being very difficult for that young man, you know. He doesn't know just yet what he wants or where he's going except that if he ever gets out he plans to reenlist."

Lawn chewed eagerly on a fingernail. "Did you give him my message?"

"Why, yes—yes, I did. I think he was very pleased. As a matter of fact, being in jail is giving that young man an excellent chance to do some thinking—some very overdue thinking. But more of that later. Are you— I mean, can you speak freely?"

Lawn looked quickly towards the kitchen, where Beulah and Jeff were making definite but diminished rattling noises indicative of dinner to come. Then she looked towards the stairs and nodded. "Free as the breeze. Helen is in her room taking a beauty sleep, and father has retired with a bottle and a book of his old press clippings. What is it? Do you want me to come into town? Because if you do, I can catch a ride in with Searles; he's just about ready to leave for the day—"

Then the girl listened for a while. Finally she said, "Yes, but I don't get it."

"Just call all of them," came the schoolteacher's clipped Bostonian accents. "The Benningtons, Mrs. Boad, Dr. Radebaugh, and Jed Nicolet. I was going to ask Adele Beale to do it for me, but she's disappeared. You know all those people as well or better than she does, anyway, and certainly better than I do."

Lawn suddenly sat up very straight, her face flushed and excited. "Of course," she said. "It takes a lot of crust, but I'll do it. If you think it will help Pat—"

Miss Withers's voice sounded pleased. "And may I suggest that you do the telephoning where you can be sure of privacy? This matter is extremely confidential, you know."

"That will be easy," Lawn promised. "Dad and Helen are avoiding me as if I had the leaping leprosy, anyway. I'll report my results later, okay?"

Hanging up, the girl rose and crossed the room to the liquor cabinet. She took up a bottle, uncorked it, and then hastily put it back, recognizing it as Scotch whiskey. She poured a jigger of brandy, took a sip, made a face, and then returned to the divan, carefully carrying the glass. "The things I do for that man!" she said to herself, and picked up the telephone again.

It was a rather longer ordeal than she had at first imagined, but she had the drawing room all to herself, without any one's disturbing her at all. Once she thought she heard an upstairs door open and steps in the hall, but when she looked up at the landing nobody was there.

Meanwhile, Pat Montague was himself in an extremely unhappy frame of mind, having just been led down the jail stairs by Officer Lunney and brought into the sheriff's office. The room was full of officers in and out of uniform, some of them old acquaintances by this time and some new. Two of them seemed to be putting the finishing touches to an electric chair, which was hooked up with something that resembled an old-fashioned crystal radio receiver.

"It isn't really the hot-squat, Montague, though I'll admit it looks a little like it," Vinge greeted him.

Pat swallowed with difficulty.

Inspector Oscar Piper came towards him. "You asked for it, so here it is. It's perfectly clear, isn't it? You are submitting to the lie-detector test willingly and of your own volition. The law says that no man can be forced to testify against himself. You want to submit to the test because you hope it will prove the truth of statements previously made by you, is that right?"

The prisoner nodded.

"You have a right to have an attorney present if you wish."

Pat shook his head. "No, thanks, Inspector."

Piper shrugged and turned to the sheriff. "I guess we can get going," he said.

And Miss Hildegarde Withers waited beside the telephone. Having dropped a stone into the pool, she sat still and let the ripples spread out to engulf her destined victim. Or was it victims?

To pass the time she picked up a magazine which contained a fascinating treatise on the genetics of tropical fish, particularly of two varieties whose normal habitat was the jungles, the *tierra caliente* of Southern Mexico. The article made clear how easy it would be to develop wagtails, albinos, comet platys, and something known as the black-bottomed wagtail platy, all from the crossbreeding of the wild swordtail and the platyfish.

She put down the book and wondered if the murder instinct could be bred out of mankind and if murderers were perhaps only sports, mutants, or throwbacks to Cain or the Neanderthal. When highly developed tropical fish mated at random the offspring reverted to the original types. Yet of course all humans mated at random, or at least according to the dictates of happenchance. Midge Beale, catching pretty, shrewish Adele on the rebound from her romance with Huntley Cairns. Helen Abbott, lonely and confused and unwilling to wait for a sweetheart in uniform, drifting into matrimony with the first man who asked her. Her father, a widower, marrying the Princess Zoraida …

The impulse to murder, Miss Withers thought, must be a recessive trait in all human beings. Why was it, then, dominant in a few? Of course Bertillon and Lombroso had believed that murderers differed in appearance from other people, but the schoolteacher knew to her sorrow that this was not true.

There was no sign, like the overlong tail fin of the swordtail cropping up in a litter of comet platys, to mark the throwback.

The schoolteacher got up and made herself a lettuce sandwich and drank a glass of milk, still carefully keeping her eyes from the telephone, on the old theory about the watched pot. She felt possessed of an inner tension which could only partially be explained by the oppressive stillness of the air.

Murderers, according to the inspector at least, were usually trapped because they could not let well enough alone. As a rule, they felt sure that they had left something undone and many times came out into the open to cover up tracks that didn't exist. The murderer of Huntley Cairns had so far avoided making this mistake, at least. Perhaps with a little teasing, a little goading, he would show himself one of these moments—to the discerning eye.

But the telephone didn't even ring once. Miss Withers thought of the bathtub, remembering the old story about the pretty girl who said that on a Saturday night she had to take three baths before the phone would ring. The not ringing of the telephone became a tangible thing, an audible sound in itself, just as the absence of the vibration of a ship's engines, when for some reason they have to be stopped at sea, can awaken every passenger.

"This is silly," decided Miss Withers. She went over to the phone, gave the Cairns number to the operator at the desk, and waited. Lawn Abbott answered immediately in her natural voice.

"Oh," she said. "Well, I didn't call you back because it was no dice. I called them, all of them, over and over again."

"You mean they won't come?"

"Nope. Nobody home. The Benningtons' maid finally answered and said they had gone out for dinner and the evening. Jed's houseboy wouldn't say anything except that Mister Nicolet was out. Harry Radebaugh has his phone connected up with a switchboard service for doctors, and they answered but wouldn't say anything except that they would have the doctor call later. I finally got hold of Trudy Boad and she said at first that her mother was out. I called back and she said her mother had gone to bed and couldn't be disturbed."

"I see." Miss Withers's plans swiftly rearranged themselves, like the pattern in a child's kaleidoscope. "It would appear that the group is holding its own convocation. I shall still try to crash the party."

"But how can you?" Lawn cried. "You don't know where—"

"They will be at somebody's house," the schoolteacher told her. "I shall simply climb into a taxicab and go exploring—to the homes of all of them. Outside one house there will be five or six cars, so that will be the meeting place. Anyway, thank you for your help. Let's hope that tonight will see the end of all this trouble."

"I wish—" the girl began, and stopped.

"Is anything wrong?" Miss Withers pressed after a moment.

"Only my sister and my father …" Lawn began. Then her tone changed. "And I'm really very sorry, but we have no comment to make and nothing whatever to say for publication. Good-bye!"

The line went dead.

"Family trouble again," Miss Withers deduced. Again she felt that there was something to be said for living alone, where one's telephone calls, entrances, and exits could be questioned by nobody. She asked the desk to summon her a taxi and headed forth into the summer twilight.

"Among the most gala social events of the summer season (according to the Shoreham *Standard*) are the justly famous evenings around the barbecue pit at the delightfully informal home of Commander and Mrs. Sam Bennington, and invitations thereto are much sought after."

Not on this particular evening. Five unhappy people were gathered together around the bare and cheerless charcoal grill at the foot of the garden. Overhead an unshaded electric bulb cast a pale and unflattering light upon the group, as well as attracting a horde of June bugs, Mayflies, gnats, and mosquitoes who had nothing else on that evening.

From the roadway, an onlooker could have seen only the glow of the light and heard only a hum of voices that now and again rose to a crescendo and then died suddenly and started all over again. There was no tinkle of ice in tall julep glasses, no sharp spat! of the ping-pong ball hit across the deserted table. Nor was there any rich, sizzling scent of charcoal-broiled beefsteaks.

Nothing was being served by Ava Bennington this evening except worry. Worry and conversation, and from the roadway Miss Hildegarde Withers couldn't hear enough of that to know what they were talking about. She explored the garage entrance, came close enough to the house to get entangled in the woven wire of an abandoned puppy run, and finally managed to mount a stone wall, crawl beneath a sagging clothes line, and find her way down the slope toward the group of people.

"Yoo-hoo!" she cried as she stumbled down upon them, her voice quavering a little as she saw the surprised hostility in their drawn, gray faces. She only hoped that she was getting closer to the secret of all this; getting warmer, as the children said.

If she was getting warmer, the five people around the outdoor grill looked cold, for all the mugginess of the night. Jed Nicolet had a wet, unlighted cigarette drooping from his mouth, and his thin fox face was a mask of perturbation. Mame Boad, wearing comfortable shoes and an uncomfortable expression, was biting thoughtfully at her pearls. Dr. Harry

Radebaugh seemed to have lost ten pounds since she had seen him last, and as for the Benningtons, they looked as if they had been washed in overhot water and shrunk a size and a half.

"I told you so," said Jed Nicolet to nobody in particular.

The schoolteacher thrashed through the last of the rosebushes and came out on the stone flagging of the patio. "I'll skip all explanations and apologies," she said. "We may as well come to the point at once. If you good people are having a meeting to decide which of you murdered Huntley Cairns, I'd like to get in on it."

There was a long, ominous silence, somehow made heavier still by the flicker of heat lightning off across the water to the north. It was Commander Bennington, true to Navy traditions, who recovered himself first. "My good woman," he began, "you appear to be under the impression—"

"I am," Miss Withers assured him. "Very, very much under the impression. May I sit down?"

Mame Boad, in spite of herself, tittered a little. Then Dr. Radebaugh, with chilly gallantry, provided a deck chair. Miss Withers sat down in it firmly. "Before we go any further," she opened up, "or before you have me thrown out of this conclave, let me say that I have a pretty fair idea of everything that has been going on, with the exception of the detail of who actually murdered Huntley Cairns, and that seems hardly more than a formality from this point on."

They all stared at her with a horrified fascination. Miss Withers began almost to enjoy herself. "I know why you came to me as a committee when I first arrived in Shoreham—Mr. Nicolet modestly remaining in the background—and what commission it was that you wanted me to undertake. When I refused, you decided to be your own detectives. That is why you accepted invitations to the Cairns housewarming and why you were huddling in the library shortly before he died. You were looking through his books for some clue as to his tastes and inclinations, all of which mystified Mr. Midge Beale very much at the time. I found all this out by roundabout methods—"

"The book," Jed Nicolet remarked. "*Oriental Moments.*"

"Exactly." Miss Withers removed the rental-library volume from her handbag and opened it to the place she had marked. "I read from Chapter Five, page sixty-two," she said. "Quote: 'It was at this dinner party at General Choy's that Manya Werenska made her classic suggestion for dealing with the Japanese in case they ever actually occupied the city. All the officers, she insisted, should be invited to lunch and then fed meatballs filled with sharp splinters of bamboo rolled up tightly and bound with some animal fiber such as bacon rind. It was a method of poisoning wolves in the Pekin hills, dating back into antiquity like everything else in China. When the digestive juices acted on the fiber, the bamboo splinter would open up and—' "

"That's enough!" cried Ava Bennington.

"It would seem to be plenty," Miss Withers agreed. "There is no need to go into the grisly details. For your further information, I was, until last fall, a dog owner myself. My wirehaired, Dempsey, died—but he died of old age."

The circle suddenly closed more tightly about her. "Can you understand," Dr. Radebaugh asked quietly, "how a man feels who brings up an English setter from puppyhood so that it's his best friend and only immediate family, and then watches it die in convulsions?"

"Your dog came home to die," Jed Nicolet said softly. "Wotan lay in the gutter all night where a hit-run driver left him."

"But he didn't die," Mame Boad cut in. "You saved him. Me, I had seven cockers racing around the place in the spring, all the finest show stock, with bloodlines that meant one of them would stand a chance as best of breed and maybe best in show at Morris and Essex. Now I have one—the runt—and I have her because she was too slow to grab the poisoned meat that some fiend threw into my yard at night."

"By 'fiend' you refer, I presume, to the late Huntley Cairns?" Miss Withers pressed.

"He ran down my dog," Nicolet put in. "I proved there were black dog hairs on his front bumper and even started suit. But he settled out of court, and for plenty."

"No doubt that made you all focus your suspicions on Cairns," Miss Withers pointed out. "But isn't there quite a difference between running over a dog in the dark and setting out to poison all the dogs in a township?"

Bennington shook his head. "Don't forget that the book was in Cairns's library. Jed Nicolet took it away with him, and he'll bear witness that there were dirty smudges on that particular page, too. My wife's poodles were saved the first time, when we pumped the arsenic out of them, but two weeks later somebody shoved some meat through a slit in the top of the car door, and that was the end of them. Peritonitis works fast, and Dr. Harvey found a sliver of bamboo in each dog."

"Bamboo—at least an American cane that has the same properties—grows as far north as this," Dr. Radebaugh pointed out. "There's a clump of it on Cairns's property."

Miss Withers nodded. "So you all brought in a mental verdict against Huntley Cairns! For that matter, none of you remembered that there were five other people in the Cairns house who had access to the library and who could have read that book and made use of the device. Six, actually, if you include the gardener, who seems to have had the run of the place."

There were flashes of heat lightning all across the eastern sky now, and the crickets and tree frogs sounded like a modern symphony heard through a curtain.

"Like most people who are fond of animals," Miss Withers went on, "I've read now and then in the newspapers about dog-poisoning epidemics, and I suppose I've said to myself that the person who would do a thing like that ought to have a dose of his own medicine. However, there is always recourse to the law—"

"Sure, sure!" cut in Jed Nicolet bitterly. "As a member of the bar, I might inform you that dog poisoners usually get off with a suspended sentence, or at worst with a nominal fine for malicious mischief. The owner can of course start a civil suit, but most juries fix the value of any dog at no more than ten dollars."

"Then the law, as Mr. Dickens had somebody say, is an ass. But all that is beside the point." Miss Withers wagged her forefinger. "You are all gathered here because you believe that one of you took the law into his own hands last Saturday—after the discovery of this book in Cairns's library—and drowned him then and there in his own swimming pool." She cocked her head. "True or false?"

Nobody needed to answer. "Which explains," went on Miss Withers, "Mr. Nicolet's effort to help Pat Montague, the innocent bystander. You are all reasonably nice people, and you wouldn't like to have an innocent man suffer for the crime you are sure one of you committed." She paused for a dramatic moment, which was spoiled by the whine of a mosquito dive-bombing her ear. "The sad part of it all, however, is this. If any one of you did murder Huntley Cairns, you got the wrong man!"

They stared at her, but nobody spoke.

"That is all, or nearly all, I came here to say," she told them. "Think it over and consult your consciences. And remember that if Huntley Cairns met his death because of the dog-poisoning epidemic in Shoreham, the whole thing was a criminal mistake!"

"Wait a minute," Commander Bennington argued. "How can you explain away the smudge on that particular page of a book in Cairns's own library?"

She smiled at him. "Cairns was a dapper, fastidious man, very careful of his person. Why should he have left smudges in the book? Isn't it more likely that someone else with access to the house picked up that volume, idly attracted by the somewhat misleading promise of its title and jacket drawing, and then stumbled on the handy, vicious method of killing animals? As a matter of fact, the same person searched the Cairns house this morning for that book, hoping to destroy it, but of course Mr. Nicolet had carried it away the other evening for evidence."

Jed Nicolet shrugged. "Suppose I did! Why are you telling us all this?"

"Simply because I think that you know, or suspect, which one of you murdered Huntley Cairns. Up to now you have kept quiet out of a mistaken loyalty, in the belief that the murder was justified. I'm telling you that it was not—that somebody else poisoned the dogs of this town—and I have a very good idea who it was!"

"Such as?" demanded Ava Bennington breathlessly.

"I'm not mentioning any names. Of course, certain inferences could be drawn from the fact that in the first phase of this poison epidemic arsenic and other poisons readily obtainable in ordinary garden and orchard sprays, such as arsenate of lead, were used. Quite naturally, after the local veterinarian performed his autopsies and started to ask questions of the local dealers about abnormal purchases of such sprays, the poisoner had to turn to something different. It appears that he found it in a book in Cairns's library. But all that is circumstantial. Observe the motive—and consider who it is in all the world that has a perpetual grievance against the whole race of dogs."

"Someone who raises cats, of course!" said Mame Boad.

"Maybe someone who was bitten by a dog in early childhood and grew up with an abnormal phobia," suggested Dr. Radebaugh.

Miss Withers shrugged her shoulders. "Perhaps. But in that list you should include a landscape gardener whose days are spent in one neverending feud with the whole canine tribe!"

They were all standing now, making a circle of blankly hostile faces. "That's all for now," said Miss Hildegarde Withers firmly. "Class dismissed!"

She turned and headed back up the slope. Let them think over what she had said, and perhaps there would be a crack in that smug suburban armor plate.

When she had reached the stone wall she looked back, but they were all standing there, eyes turned up the slope, as if they were expecting to see her climb astride a broomstick and take off into the sky.

CHAPTER TWELVE

On the way back Miss Withers changed her mind, or at least altered it slightly after her fashion. "I believe, young man, I'd like to stop off at the Cairns house," she told the driver.

"Okay with me," he assured her jovially. "As long as that little old meter keeps ticking. You know, you're getting to be about my best customer. I sure hope you're on an expense account."

"I only wish I were," she admitted.

"You mean you're doing all this sleuthing for free?" he demanded, looking over his shoulder. "Anyway, lady, it's a waste of time. When a guy gets murdered, all you gotta do is lock up his wife. Or vice versus, as the case may be.

"A cynical but realistic attitude," the schoolteacher observed. "That's the way the police usually think, I must admit."

"Sure. Take my own case. My old lady went over the hill with my bank account before I was out of boot camp. I'd have given her the deep-six if I coulda got a furlough then, but I cooled off in time. But now in this Cairns killing, the way I figure it, they ought to have Mrs. Cairns locked up instead of that young guy. Or her father, even. That old goat would split a nickel lengthwise to avoid giving more than the exact ten-per-cent tip."

"Oh, then, Mr. Thurlow Abbott is a customer of yours?"

"Lady, when there's only two hacks in the village, everybody's a customer at one time or another. I've even hauled Mr. Cairns when his own car was in the shop and his wife or her sister had the other one. Him and Mr. Abbott had a good argument in this heap one night—"

"Really?" Miss Withers was elaborately casual. "Too bad you didn't overhear what it was about."

"I did." The driver turned into the Cairns driveway, stopped, and climbed out to scrub at his windshield, well plastered with dead bugs. "At least I heard Cairns say something about business, and Thurlow Abbott piped up in that raspy voice of his and said that Cairns wouldn't have had any business if it wasn't for him. Want me to wait, ma'am?"

"As usual," she sighed, and went up the steps to ring the bell. She had to bear on it three times before there was any answer, but finally it opened a crack and she saw the sepia face of Beulah, which broadened into a smile.

"'Evening, Miss Withers."

"Is Miss Lawn Abbott at home? I'd like to see her."

The girl hesitated. "Well, she is, and she isn't."

"Just as a favor to me, Mrs. MacTavish, can't you elaborate?"

That won a wider smile. "Miss Lawn locked herself in her room, and she won't answer when anybody knocks, because I took her up some dinner on a tray."

"You don't suppose that something might have happened to her?"

Beulah shook her head. "I wouldn't worry about that, ma'am. She had the radio on loud for a while, and now she's playing records, like she usually does when she has an argument with her sister or her father. Symphonies, mostly—all heavy, sad music. Listen!"

Sure enough, the schoolteacher could hear the throbbing beat and rumble of a symphonic orchestra, mostly basses and brasses, filtering through a closed door or two. "Jeff says she blows off steam that way," the girl went on. "Only if she's going to play so you can hear it all over the house, I wish she'd play something cheerfuller."

"Possibly," suggested Miss Withers, "she does it to annoy Mrs. Cairns and her father."

"But they aren't at home. They've gone to La Guardia Field."

"What? You mean they've left—"

"They didn't take any suitcases," Beulah interrupted quickly. "I think they just went to meet somebody, but I don't know who."

"Thank you very much. You've been most helpful."

"Anything at all," Beulah said.

"Anything? Then just tell me why you've dropped the plantation ac-cent—the 'yessums' and 'Ah sho do honeychile' patois." Miss Withers cocked her head inquisitively.

The girl hesitated. "Well, you see—that sort of talk goes with the job, like wearing an apron. In service, most homes, you've got to Uncle-Tom it. Only Jeff and I are quitting at the end of the month. Mr. Cairns left us a quarter's pay in his will, and with that and what Jeff can get under the veterans' bill of rights, he's going back to college."

"How nice for you both!" Then Miss Withers frowned. "And I don't suppose you happen to know any of the other provisions of the will?"

"Honestly, I don't," Beulah admitted. "Except about the trust. I heard Mr. Abbott say that Mrs. Cairns gets the income from that as long as she doesn't remarry."

"Very interesting. Thank you again." Miss Withers went back to her taxi. "Next stop, I believe, should be the police station," she told him. On the way back to town he made one or two tentative efforts to start the conversational ball rolling, but she barely answered him.

At the station she paid him off, wincing slightly at the amount, and marched inside. For once the officer at the desk seemed glad to see her. "Oh, Miss Withers! The inspector's been trying to phone you. We called your hotel, but you weren't there."

"Well, I'm here now," she said.

There was some delay in locating the inspector, but finally he came down the hall, a dank, dead cigar clamped in his jaws and beads of perspiration on his scalp and forehead.

"Well, look who's here!" he greeted her. He sounded, she thought, both triumphant and uneasy.

"I understand that you telephoned me, Oscar."

"Sure. Didn't I promise that you'd be the first to know?"

She peered at him. "Oscar Piper, what are you talking about?"

"Montague's confession, of course."

"His confession of *what*?"

"Everything. The works."

The world was spinning around her. "You mean that after you'd trapped him with the lie detector he broke down?"

The inspector looked carefully at his cigar, decided it was past saving, and threw it into the wastebasket beside the desk. "Not exactly. Just between us, I'll admit that the results we got with the lie detector weren't so hot. Montague showed a guilty reaction to some of the key questions about the murder of Cairns, but to some he didn't. And there were other questions tucked away in the list, like why did he kidnap Charley Ross and where did he and Jesse James hide the gold they got out of the Gallatin

Bank and what was his mother's real maiden name, and he gave a guilty reaction to those too! Maybe there was a short or something in the machine. I told you I didn't think too much of those contraptions. But, anyway, after we'd fooled around with that for a while, Montague finally gave in and began to dictate a confession. It's being typed out now for him to sign."

"With a promise of clemency?"

"That's up to Loomis, the Knight's County district attorney. He's here now, and he says he won't ask the death penalty, anyway, as there's no premeditation that can be proved."

Miss Withers looked very displeased. "Sometimes I think that we're slipping back into the dark ages of the eighteenth century, when all the police ever tried to do in solving a murder was to torture a confession out of somebody—"

"Relax, Hildegarde. There wasn't any of the rubber-hose-in-the-back-room stuff used on Montague."

"Just a two-hundred-watt bulb right in his eyes, and everybody taking turns yelling at him, which is about the same thing. Oscar, I don't know what to say. This changes everything."

The inspector looked surprised. "But I thought you knew it and that you'd rushed down here to congratulate me! It was all announced on the radio around eight o'clock—a little prematurely, but Sheriff Vinge likes to stand in well with the press and the radio newscasters, so he handed it out."

"What I actually came down here for, Oscar, was to ask you to rearrest Joe Searles."

"The Cairnses' gardener?" Piper thought that was very funny. "When did you get that bee in your bonnet?"

"Never mind. I've been thinking things over, that's all. If you won't arrest Searles, won't you at least assign a detective to watch him?"

"Relax, Hildegarde! We've got a confession—"

"And you think it will hold up?"

He hesitated only a moment. "Honestly, Hildegarde, I think so. I don't see why not. The district attorney is in there with Sheriff Vinge now, and we're going to give Montague a new lie-detector test based on his confession, just to make everything watertight."

"And is the prisoner willing to do that?"

"He's willing to do anything and everything. I never saw a man bust up into so many pieces under a load of guilt. Take it easy, Hildegarde, and don't talk yourself into thinking that this is necessarily one of those twisted, complex cases. I'll admit that in the past you've kibitzed on some murder cases that were pretty queer. But don't forget that for every one of those, we have a dozen where the homicide squad arrests the most likely suspect, proves a case against him, and eventually gets a conviction."

"Uh-huh," said Miss Withers absently.

"And remember that Pat Montague had a motive to kill Huntley Cairns, and so far nobody else did. Not even your friend the gardener, Searles."

Miss Withers didn't answer that. Just then a big, handsome, blonde girl came down the hall carrying a sheaf of typewritten manuscript. "There comes the D.A.'s secretary with the confession now," he said excitedly. "She's going into Vinge's office."

"Oscar," began Miss Withers slowly, "I think I ought to tell you—"

"Sure, sure. I've got to run along. We've got to work out a list of questions to throw at Pat Montague when he's hooked up to the lie detector."

"Then ask him one for me," suggested the schoolteacher tartly. "Ask him if he thinks a gentleman is in honor-bound to confess himself right into the electric chair for the sake of a lady he used to be in love with!"

She stalked out of the place, slamming the screen door behind her, and was morose all the way back to the hotel. Arriving at her cottage, she turned on all the lights, including the fluorescent lamp over the tank of tropical fish, but for once that watery wonder world had no power to distract or inspire her. Another fish or two seemed to be missing, but she was past caring about that.

"It must be that I have lost my grip," she said out loud. It wasn't so much that she begrudged the inspector his little triumph and his easily won confession. She had her own private opinion about the value of confessions, anyway.

Only it seemed that things were moving in the wrong direction. Currents were flowing backward. Even her fabled intuition was all haywire. Perhaps the inspector was right and she should have stayed retired. Yet away down in the back of her mind little red lights were flashing off and on, and they seemed to be spelling out a name.

On a sudden impulse she picked up the local telephone book. Sure enough, there was the name—"Searles, Joseph—Lndscpg—24 Pier Lane—4439." Evidently he needed a phone in his business. She could, she thought, find out if the man was at home, explaining the call by saying that she needed some rosebushes pruned.

Miss Withers gave the number to the hotel operator and waited. But the lie about the rosebushes was not to rest upon her conscience. "They don't answer," the operator said. "You want me to keep on trying?"

"Never mind," said the schoolteacher. Perhaps landscape gardeners kept later hours than she had imagined, for it was after eleven.

She sat down and tried to read but found that she was going over the same paragraph again and again, without the slightest idea as to its meaning. Somehow she killed time until almost twelve and tried again.

"Still no answer," the operator said.

Miss Withers frowned. Certainly a man who had to get up with the birds should be home and in bed by now. "Hold on until somebody answers," she requested. She counted as she heard the ringing sounds— eleven—twelve—thirteen.

And then, miraculously, there came a click at the other end of the line and a gruff "Wha'?"

"Is this Mr. Searles? This is Miss Withers speaking. I have some rosebushes—"

The voice at the other end of the line, heavy with sleep and alcohol, said briefly what she could do with her rosebushes, and the instrument was hung up with a crash.

"Well!" said Miss Hildegarde Withers to herself. "That nasty old man ought to have his mouth washed out with green soap!"

She stalked across the room and back again. "I certainly never in my life—"

Then she sat down suddenly in a chair and drew a deep breath. What if her bombshell dropped among the group at the Benningtons' had not proved a dud after all? What if it had bounced right into her own lap? Her accusation of Joe Searles had been almost purely rhetorical, to prove her point. But gardeners did have access to all sorts of poisons, and Searles was a dirty old man whose thumb might very well have smudged any book he was reading. Moreover, she had never in her life heard a gardener speak a good word for dogs, who were always befouling lawns and racing across new seedings and digging holes in flowerbeds to bury ancient bones salvaged from garbage cans.

But granting all that, then why not take the next, obvious step? Suppose that Huntley Cairns had suspected his employee, or even found him out? A man with a wholesale disregard for canine life might not stop at taking human life. And who but a gardener and household handyman could easier assemble some neat little device which would splice one rake handle on to another, forming a shaft that would reach far down into the water, to the very bottom of the deep end of the swimming pool?

Then he could have slipped away to dispose of the gadget and return to discover the body—only with the added luck of discovering Pat Montague on the spot?

This was, she decided, too big a thing to handle alone. The more she thought about it, the more convinced she was that Searles had killed Huntley Cairns in order to protect himself from exposure and arrest as the fiend who had brought death to half the canine population of Shoreham and aroused the furious owners.

She grabbed the telephone and put through a call for the inspector, but was told by the man at the police station desk that Piper was in an important conference and could not be disturbed. They would tell him that she had called.

And that was that. Miss Withers stalked up and down the room for a few moments, like some weird, ungainly bird of prey—a very, very nervous bird. In the movies at a time like this it was always the heroine—and she still thought of herself in that light—who went rushing off alone to beard the murderer in his den. That always led up to the scare sequence in the lonely old house on the moors, or in the mad scientist's laboratory, or—this season—in the private mental hospital of the celebrated but too-handsome psychiatrist.

"If I had but known the terror that awaited me—" was usually one of the lines of dialogue.

The whole thing could, of course, wait until morning. Meanwhile poor Pat Montague, to whom she had once done a considerable injustice, was being put to the question by means of lie detectors and third degrees by district attorneys and country sheriffs and the inspector himself. Heaven knew to what lengths they would go to squeeze just the right kind of confession out of him.

Besides, tonight Joe Searles was drunk and asleep. Miss Withers did not put too much faith in the ancient phrase about *in vino veritas*, but she did know that a man suddenly awakened from sleep is psychologically incapable of telling a good lie. His mental defenses were all down, and it took time to set them up again.

According to the ancient gold watch pinned to her bosom, it was almost the witching hour of twelve. Miss Withers put on her hat again, took up her umbrella, and was about to head out into the night when the telephone rang.

With a sudden sigh of relief she seized upon it and cried, "Oscar! Hallo!"

Only it wasn't Oscar, it was Lawn Abbott, and her voice was hushed, a little strained. "They shoved a note under my door a while ago—that you'd stopped by. Anything wrong?"

"Almost everything," Miss Withers admitted. "What I stopped by to tell you was that I crashed the meeting and dropped my bomb. But that doesn't seem to matter now. Or hadn't you heard? Pat Montague has confessed."

"That's a lie!" came the girl's voice in an angry whisper.

"I'm afraid not," Miss Withers said a little stiffly. "I had it straight from the best sources."

"I mean the confession is a lie, no matter what Pat said!" Lawn was fiercely confident.

"Oh! Well, I agree with you. I think that the murderer lies in an entirely different direction. I was just about to start out, in the hope of making a surprise attack. Care to play Watson to my Sherlock?"

"Love to. But where, and how?"

"I intend to call on Mr. Joe Searles at once," Miss Withers told her. There was a strange gulp at the other end of the wire. "What?"

"Nothing. I just swallowed a damn. You see, I'm afraid I can't get into town. Helen and father went off somewhere earlier—I think they took both cars, and if they didn't, still Helen has the keys to the roadster. My sister and I aren't on very good terms. I could try to catch a ride—or—"

"Never mind," Miss Withers said.

"But I'd like to … Oops! I hear somebody coming. More trouble." The receiver clicked.

" 'So I'll do it myself,' said the little red hen," observed the schoolteacher. Emerging from her cottage, she found both taxis away on calls. Searles's address, however, should lie within walking distance, almost on the edge of town and near the shore. She set out sturdily, her sensible heels tapping on the side walks like drumsticks.

It was a pleasant, reassuring sound at first, and then it seemed to grow louder in the stillness, so that the repetitive tap-tap-tap filled the narrowing streets and echoed from the walls and buildings. The street lights seemed to grow dimmer and farther apart.

It was a very silent night. Once or twice an automobile rushed past her, making everything quieter by contrast. Far away a dog barked, and there was the lonely, banshee wail of a railroad engine's whistle, drawn thin by distance.

She found herself walking on the brightest side of the street, and— since she could not whistle satisfactorily—humming to herself. At last she understood what Officer Lunney had meant about the difference between a criminal type and a solid citizen on a lonely street at night, and the way each acted when an officer appeared. She would certainly have given any one in uniform a hearty greeting and probably tried to engage the man in conversation besides, only tonight there was no sign of a patrolman.

The street lights ended, but the street kept on, and so did Miss Withers. Pier Lane turned out to be an unpaved alley leading off to the right, but she determinedly trod its sandy ruts, beneath ancient signs promising "All Kinds Baits" and "Used Marine Hardware and Gear," until she was brought up short against a whitewashed picket fence. There was a station wagon parked in the side yard, its dead headlights softly reflecting the lights of the town like a pair of blind eyes, so this must be the place.

Miss Withers came softly up a board sidewalk towards the front door of the one-story shack, her umbrella held like a lance. Then she relaxed. There was no danger of a watchdog here, at least. She came up on the porch, littered with garden tools and old rubber hose, and approached the door on tiptoe.

Even with the help of the tiny pencil flashlight in her purse she could see neither bell nor knocker. She took a deep breath, made a fist, and knocked sharply.

The little building seemed to roar and rattle with the sound, but nobody answered. Then Miss Withers caught her breath, for the door had been ajar and now it was softly swinging inward. She sniffed sharply, trying to classify the scents which poured out of the pitch-blackness.

"Alcohol," she whispered. "Fish … tobacco … cabbage … hamburger …" But was there something else, something more subtle, more frightening?

She cast the thin gleam of the flashlight into the room so that it played over walls decorated with pages torn from the Sunday supplements, over a stove and table crowded with dirty pans and dishes, across a floor marked with a wide, dark stain.

The stain came from behind a couch on which Joe Searles was lying, his stockinged feet sticking out all akimbo. He was still in his overalls, and his hands clutched the tangled blankets in a frozen spasm of agony.

"Mr. Searles!" she whispered once, and tiptoed forward. She started to breathe more easily when she saw that the stain on the floor was only water. Then she found that the water had overflowed from a full pail of water standing on the floor at the end of the couch. The reason it had overflowed was that Joe Searles's head had been shoved down, jammed tight into the pail, and left there.

The pail had a capacity of four gallons, but he was as dead as if he had been at the bottom of all the seven seas.

CHAPTER THIRTEEN

The immediate requirement, Miss Withers decided, was more light on the subject. She finally found and pulled the dirty string which turned on the glaring overhead bulb, and then looked at the old-fashioned gold watch pinned to her old-fashioned bosom and noted that it was just seventeen minutes past twelve.

The important thing was to keep perfectly calm. After all, there was no real reason why her knees should be quaking or her throat too dry to swallow. This was, she reassured herself, an amateur detective's dream come true, because here was a still-warm corpse and a murder room unsullied and untrampled by the myrmidons of the police, its clues crying to heaven to be discovered.

It was really only a matter of where to begin. Looking for clues in this cottage was going to be on the difficult side, she realized. The place was disordered, but it appeared to be a disorder of long standing. The door had been left ajar, but there was nothing to show that the murderer had entered or left that way, for both the rear windows were open, and one of them was unscreened.

True, there were a few footprints damply imprinted on the linoleum. But, she thought, it would have been simpler if there had been an exotic Turkish cigarette still burning in the ashtray. There was not, however, even an ashtray, as Searles had evidently smoked a pipe and let the refuse fall where it may. There wasn't even an initialed gold cuff-link glistening on the floor, or a scented lace handkerchief clutched in the dead man's hand. She thought of looking through Searles's pockets and then backed down. It had seemed ghoulish enough to approach the pail and lift his head so that she could be sure that it was Searles and that he was beyond help.

There was a great deal of difference, Miss Withers was discovering, between standing on the sidelines and gently heckling the police as they performed their routine investigation, and trying to work all by her lonesome.

More than that, she still felt jittery, although Joe Searles was certainly past harming any one. And she knew that the murderer would be anywhere else in the world besides in the neighborhood of his deed. All the same, she tiptoed over to the antique bathroom and peered within, surprising some cockroaches and a beetle or so, and then looked into the clothes closet, which contained nothing except the dead man's Sunday suit of shiny serge. An empty holster hung nearby on a nail.

At the other end of the room was the alcove fitted out as a kitchen, and this she found more to her liking as a spot for scientific deduction. The first notation she made was that Searles had dined that night upon hamburger patties, fried potatoes mixed with onions, rye bread with bacon grease as a substitute for butter, and a bottle of beer.

"The condemned man ate a hearty meal," she observed softly. Worst of all, she had a feeling that it was dollars to doughnuts that she herself had condemned him, however unwittingly. She decided, after a close study of the remains of the meal and the hardness of the grease on the dishes, that Searles had eaten early in the evening. She made a most detailed inspection of the cupboards and shelves and then looked into the garbage can, which sadly needed emptying. From that Miss Withers turned her attention to the wastepaper basket, which held several daily newspapers, metropolitan and local, with all wordage on the Cairns murder clipped out, also some onion peels, the bloodstained paper in which the hamburger had been wrapped, and an empty beer bottle. She emptied all this trash out upon the newspaper, having other uses for the basket.

Miss Withers was holding a container of pancake flour in her hand when she first heard the sound of the car turning into the alley. Her first natural feminine impulse was to lock herself into the bathroom and scream, but then she noticed that the approaching automobile had a red spotlight and that as it stopped two men got out with a flash of brass buttons.

"Oh, dear!" cried the schoolteacher as she turned out the light somewhat tardily. But by the time the two officers from the police radio car were crowding into the doorway, guns out and flashlights blazing, she was calmly seated at the telephone, dialing the number of the Shoreham police station. "I'd like to speak to Inspector Oscar Piper," she was saying. "I want to report a murder—"

That call was doomed from the start never to be completed. But as Miss Withers tried to explain to the inspector some time later, it was the officer's own fault if he tripped over the wastebasket. "Because he needn't have been in so much of a hurry to snatch the phone away from me when I was only trying to report the murder!"

They were standing now on the porch of Searles's cottage, where until a moment or two ago the maiden schoolteacher had been in police custody. Inside the cottage there was now a considerable hubbub going on, with much flickering of flashlights and the rumble of official masculine voices, where Joe Searles had taken on in death an importance that could never have been his in life.

"Just relax, Hildegarde," the inspector said patiently. "I want you to answer one or two questions. Why did you put the wastebasket in front of the door?"

She sniffed. "Because of the flour, of course."

"I see. That makes it simple. Thanks very much. It's just as clear as crystal to me now. And do you mind telling me why you poured all that pancake flour on the floor?"

"Your men coming so belatedly to arrest Searles startled me. I only meant to put down a little flour."

"A little flour! But for God's sake, why?"

"Go blow on it, and see," she told him.

The inspector peered at her, his eyes suddenly sharp and fixed with a new worry. "Hildegarde, are you feeling all right? We'd better get you home—"

"Oh, stop it! I'm not out of my mind. I asked you to go blow on the spilled flour, just as I told you. You see, I poured the flour on the clearest footprint. The murderer must have stepped into the water that overflowed from the pail when he stuck Searles's head in. It was evaporating very fast, and I didn't see how else to protect it, so I poured the flour over it and then put the wastebasket on top."

"The idea being, if I may ask?"

"A reverse-action *moulage*, of a sort. I thought that perhaps the flour would stick to the damp spot and give the outline of the footprint."

The inspector suddenly left her and hurried inside. After a moment there was the sound of flapping newspaper, and then Sheriff Vinge's voice. "There she is, damn if she ain't. Come here, you with the camera. And who's got the tape measure?"

After some time the inspector came back out on the porch, mopping his brow. "It's a man's shoe, medium-narrow toe, size 8½ B," he admitted. "That ought to be of some help, unless, as the sheriff just suggested, you made the print yourself—"

"Does that look like an 8½ B?" demanded the schoolteacher, exposing her stout oxford and a thin if slightly bony ankle. He shook his head. "And," she continued, "just where does Sheriff Vinge come in on this case? Isn't it out of his jurisdiction?"

Piper shook his head. "City or country, it's all the same. The local chief of police is a political relic, seventy years old, and Vinge operates as deputy chief. He seems inclined to take the reins back in his own hands—I guess he doesn't like the way I'm handling things. As a matter of fact, I don't like the way I'm handling things either." The inspector broke off as a stubby, competent-looking little man came out of the door, jamming a straw hat down over his bald head. "Oh, Doctor!"

The inspector introduced them. "Dr. Farney, can you tell us anything about the time of death?"

"Not much. His body temperature's 97.5, which on a night like this means he's been dead not more than two hours and not less than half an hour. It's just a case of simple drowning—a man can drown in a pail or an inch-deep puddle, for that matter, just as easy as in an ocean."

"I see. Any chance of suicide or accident?"

The doctor stuck out his lower lip. "Can't rule out the possibility. But offhand I'd say that somebody jammed the man's head under water and held it there."

"Which would mean, wouldn't it," Miss Withers excitedly put in, "that the murderer must have been an exceptionally powerful man?"

Farney was openly amused. "I think, ma'am, that you yourself could have done it if you were mad enough. You see, Searles was asleep, apparently in a drunken stupor. He was unconscious before he knew what was happening to him."

"And you can't narrow the time element down any?" Piper asked.

Dr. Farney shook his head. "Well, I can!" insisted Miss Withers. Both men turned to stare at her. "Because I called Searles on the phone a few minutes before twelve—it rang and rang and rang and finally he answered. And I discovered the body at twelve-seventeen."

"You phoned Searles?" Piper demanded. "But why?"

"I was worried," she admitted. "I felt that earlier this evening I had started something, and I didn't know what. I was sure that Searles hadn't told all he knew, so I phoned him. When he answered his voice was thick, and his language—"

The inspector said dryly that he could understand about Searles's language after being awakened at midnight. "You recognized his voice?"

She shrugged. "It sounded like Searles, only his voice was all gummy and thick."

The doctor agreed that that would be natural, with Searles in the besotted condition in which he had gone to sleep. "It's a wonder he woke up at all," Farney continued. "Well, if you'll excuse me—"

"Wait, Doctor," the inspector said. "How soon can you post him?"

"Why—won't he keep?" Dr. Farney scowled. "I've got to take out kids' tonsils all morning. How about getting another man—young Radebaugh or somebody?"

Miss Withers jabbed the inspector sharply with her elbow, and as he turned in surprised indignation the doctor settled the problem by giving in. "Oh, all right, I'll do it as soon as you can get the body up town. Medicos aren't supposed to need any sleep, anyway." Mumbling quietly to himself, Dr. Farney hurried off towards his car.

"Just a minute, Hildegarde," the inspector said. "I'll see if Vinge has ordered the ambulance yet. Don't go away, I want to talk to you."

He was back in a moment. "I want to talk to you, Oscar. I want to explain why I came over here—" She broke off as she found that he had taken her arm and was leading her down the steps.

"Tell me on the way back," he said. "I want to get you out of here before Vinge arrests you for the murder."

"Why—" she gasped.

"You have a talent for getting into trouble," he went on. "How'd you know Searles was going to be killed?"

"But I didn't! I thought he was the murderer, and I was going to surprise him into a confession——" She smiled. "Don't look so glum and disgusted, Oscar. Because this second murder proves one thing, anyway. Pat Montague is innocent."

They came out of the alleyway, away from the slow hushing sound of the breakers on the shore. The inspector laughed bitterly. "You may as well know all," he said. "We let Montague loose a little after eleven o'clock."

Miss Withers gasped again. "But, Oscar!"

"We had to. The confession was no good at all. As soon as he signed it we put him back under the lie detector and it all fell to pieces. Not one thing in the confession was on the level, except that he hated Cairns and wanted him dead. Of course, he may have been tricking the machine, but that's awfully roundabout."

"But, Oscar, isn't it true that when the machine does give a false reading it is because the suspect has built up a false sense of guilt about unimportant things, in a way hypnotized himself into concealing things that don't matter so he'll confuse the issue?"

"Something like that. Anyway, we were up a tree. Then finally Loomis, the D.A., suggested that we forget the lie detector and try a truth serum, or whatever you call it."

"Not that scopolamine stuff again?"

"No, twilight sleep is out of date. We were talking about that new drug they developed in the Army medical corps to loosen up the subconscious of bad cases of battle fatigue. When anybody's had enough sodium betapentalin he'll answer questions truthfully, he can't help it. Only—"

"Only Pat Montague refused his permission?"

"Permission hell. There's a new type of the drug you can give through the mouth, in coffee or anything. Taste's faintly salty, like all pentothalic derivatives, that's all. We were going to try it on Montague first and ask his permission later. By that time maybe we'd better have had a real confession instead of a fake one like he gave us earlier."

"But even so, could you use it?"

"Not in court. But we figured we'd have enough of the real facts so we could prove our case, anyway. I even had the chief medical examiner send me out some of the stuff"—here Piper showed her a small blue glass bottle—"but we never got to use it."

"Still insisting that Montague is guilty?" she interrupted. "Can't you ever forget that blessed triangle of yours?"

He smiled. "There are new angles to the triangle now. And Searles's death doesn't make things any simpler, either. On the contrary, as a matter of fact." They both turned to watch the ambulance as it sped along on its mission to pick up what was left of the unhappy gardener.

"But if you were so convinced of Montague's guilt—"

"Listen a minute," Piper said. "Look, Hildegarde. We never held Montague for murder, but just for investigation, see? But what do you think Mrs. Helen Cairns up and does yesterday? She telegraphs to Chicago for a hotshot criminal lawyer, meets him at the airport, and rushes him over to the station, stopping to see a judge on the way. So all of a sudden we had this stew-bum of a wild Irishman on our hands—"

Miss Withers began to smile. "Clarence Darrow, Fallon, or Earl Rogers?"

"None of them. Some guy named Malone or Mahoney. Before we even knew he was in town he'd got wise to the betapentalin gag, uncovered the sheriff's private bottle of rye, dated up the D.A.'s big blonde secretary, and slapped a writ of habeas corpus in Vinge's face."

They walked on in silence. "A fast worker," Miss Withers said.

"Jim the Penman crossed with Captain Kidd," remarked the inspector bitterly. "Anyway, he sprung his client about eleven, which gave Montague plenty of time to kill Searles, who was the only real witness against him."

"But if Montague went off in the company of his lawyer and Helen Cairns, then he has an alibi—"

"He didn't. He went off alone, like a bat out of hell. Last I saw of Mr. Whatshisname, he was sitting in Vinge's office, figuring up an expense account for Mrs. Cairns and singing some silly song about how he caught himself a midnight train and beat his way to Georgia."

"But wasn't Helen waiting outside for Pat?"

"In the hall—but he went out the side door, without a word of thanks to the hotshot lawyer or a good-bye to anybody. She hung around a while and then drove off alone, looking mad as a wet hen."

"My, my," said Miss Withers. "It must have been a great disappointment to Helen Cairns. After she'd gone to all that trouble—"

"For two cents I'd run the stew-bum out of town," Piper growled. "I've got a hunch he isn't entitled to practice before the New York bar, anyway."

"I'm afraid, Oscar, that you have even worse worries than that. Or rather you will have in a minute, when I get up courage enough to make a sort of confession." By this time they were coming up the clamshell-bordered path towards her door. "Please come inside and I'll make you some coffee."

"Haven't time, thanks," Piper said. "Now what's this about a confession? You're not going to tell me that you did Searles in, are you?"

The amusement went out of his face as he saw her expression. "I'm afraid," she said, "that I did just that. You'd better change your mind and come in."

The inspector came in and even accepted a cup of warmed-over coffee, but he was too much on edge to drink it. "Go ahead and tell me the worst," he demanded.

"I meant it for the best. How was I to know? I mean, I was only trying to help uncover the trail by smoking out something that seemed rotten in Denmark, and—"

"Will you please stop the sansifrans double talk?"

She took a deep breath and began again. "Oscar, do you remember your promising to try to find out for me just what it was that a certain committee of local citizens had approached me about when I first came to Shoreham?"

He nodded impatiently, took a sip of his coffee, and burned his mouth. "Damn and blast! Sorry, go on."

"I found out for myself. I also found out, through the help of the Beales' talkativeness, that the local committee had been trying to go ahead with its own sleuthing. You see, they were trying to find out who had been poisoning dogs hereabouts, and they had come to the conclusion that it was Huntley Cairns because of something they found in his library just before he was murdered. There seemed a very good chance that one of them—or more than one—had immediately taken matters into his own hands and had drowned Cairns in his own pool."

"If that's all you have to say, forget it. People don't commit murder to avenge the poisoning of a pup." He started to rise.

"Wait, Oscar. Not normal people. But just who is normal these days? There's always an aftermath of hysteria after a major war, and on top of that the atom bombs didn't just blow up two Japanese cities; they blew the foundations out from under every one of us. Everybody is jittery. And you yourself know that the files are full of cases where murder was committed over a few dollars, or because a neighbor insisted on mowing his lawn too early on a Sunday morning, or because a husband misunderstood his wife's psychic one-club bid in a hot rubber of bridge."

He shrugged. "Go on—get to the point, will you?"

"I shall. So I decided that while one or two of the people in that group might have murdered Cairns, they couldn't all be in on it. And the rest must be feeling worried and guilty and ready to crack. I tried to get them all together and then learned that they themselves were having a meeting to discuss the mess they were in. So I walked into the meeting and I dropped what I hoped was a bombshell. I told them I knew all, or nearly all—and that if Cairns had been killed for that reason, then they had got the wrong man, because he hadn't been the dog poisoner at all. In proving my case I'm afraid I let them think that I had evidence enough to prove that the real dog poisoner was Joe Searles."

Piper set the coffee down on a nearby table. "I begin to see."

"I hope you do—and that you'll understand. Anyway, after I'd done that I got to worrying—suppose Searles was really the murderer and had killed his employer to cover up the dog poisoning? I talked myself into believing him guilty, and finally I very rashly went down there hoping to surprise him into a confession, and I found him dead!"

"And you have a very good idea that somebody in the group, on learning they'd got the wrong man the first time, up and rushed off to get the right one!"

She nodded. "It seems logical."

"So now it's a question of whether Mrs. Boad, or the Benningtons, or Nicolet, or Doc Radebaugh wears a size-8½-B shoe!" Piper brightened a little at the prospect of something definite to get his teeth into. He even finished his coffee. "You've really made a mess of things this time, trying to work alone in the dark—but maybe I can still save something out of it, with that footprint to go on."

"Yes, Oscar, but——"

He paused in the doorway. "Don't worry about it too much. I'll see you in the morning. We may even have the case all washed up—"

"Yes, perhaps. If it only wasn't for the other clue in Searles's cottage tonight!"

"The other—what other?"

"The whiskey bottle," she pointed out softly.

"But there wasn't any whiskey bottle!"

"To quote from the esteemed Mr. Holmes, 'That was the curious incident!' The man had been drinking—the place smelled of it—but obviously he hadn't spent the evening in any bar. And why the killer should bother to carry away a whiskey bottle——"

The inspector thought and then shrugged. "Searles probably threw it out of the window in a drunken moment."

She looked dubious. "Perhaps. And perhaps he brought his rotgut liquor home with him in a brown paper bag, but I doubt it. The more I think about this case, Oscar, the more I am convinced that from the beginning we have been looking for the strange and fantastic, when the actual truth is very plain and simple. As plain as—"

"As the nose on your face?" The inspector beat her to that one and then got out of the door before she could think of a reply.

" 'He laughs best …' " murmured the schoolteacher to herself. She took a small blue glass bottle from her handbag and studied it thoughtfully. It had been very easy to abstract it from the inspector's coat pocket as they walked along. The idea of an otherwise harmless drug which would force a tongue to speak the truth was extremely attractive to her at the moment.

The question was—how to use it? For truth was, she knew, a double-edged sword.

CHAPTER FOURTEEN

The sun rose next morning above a bank of clouds a little after six, and so, through no fault of her own, did Miss Hildegarde Withers. She was rudely summoned out of a deep though troubled slumber to hear a heavy hammering upon her front door.

"Just a minute!" she called, arraying herself hastily in a bathrobe. She rushed to the door and then relaxed when she saw that it was only the inspector, looking, she thought, even more gray and worn than was his usual wont. "Why, Oscar, you said you'd drop over in the morning, but this seems just the middle of the night!"

He stared at her, unsmiling, and she realized that he had something on his mind. "Well, don't just stand there! Tell me what's happened, for heaven's sake. It's not another murder is it?"

"No. But you'd better get dressed as quick as you can."

She promised that she wouldn't be a minute, insisted that he come in and sit down, and then disappeared into the bedroom. The inspector came inside, but he did not sit down. He stalked up and down the room, looking at his watch every few minutes.

Miss Withers appeared, dressed and combed, sooner than he had expected. "There!" she said. "I gather that you aren't even giving me time for breakfast? Let us go then—and don't tell me where, since you seem to enjoy being so secretive about it." She chose a hat which looked rather like a last year's bird's nest and planted it firmly upon her head.

"You'd better pack an overnight bag too," Piper told her.

"But, Oscar—"

He turned wearily towards her. "You may as well know. It's none of my doing, and I guess I could have handled Vinge, but the district attorney insisted that you be taken into technical custody as a material witness in the death of Joe Searles. Loomis didn't think much of your little bombshell that you dropped on the group at Benningtons' last night."

Her sniff was like a snort. "I see! So I'm to be locked up, and the murderer goes free—"

"I doubt it. We've ordered everybody down at Vinge's office at seven o'clock, and when I say everybody I mean everybody. This second killing has blown the lid wide open, and anything goes. So pack your toothbrush—I've got a car waiting."

She fussed with a small suitcase and then crossed the room to bend over the aquarium. "I'm afraid," the inspector told her, "that you can't take those fish along with you."

"That wasn't my idea. But if they're to be abandoned here indefinitely …" She sniffed, and lifted the top of the tank, sprinkling powdered fish food into the glass triangle which floated on top of the tepid water.

Instantly the entire happy family of fancy fish swarmed out of the plant forest, plunging enthusiastically into the falling column of manna from heaven. Even the snails, catfish, and dojos hastened towards the rock-bordered depression in the center of the tank's floor to see what would settle down their way. They ranged themselves at the bottom, goggling upward.

"Take your time," Inspector Piper said in a low voice. "I've only got two murders to solve today, and I mean today. I'll be shipped back to Centre Street with my tail between my legs if I don't have this case signed, sealed, and delivered by then."

But Miss Withers was at the moment paying him very little attention. "My female *betta* is missing," she cried. "And so is the angelfish Gabriel. Or Gabrielle—nobody would know or care except another angelfish—"

"I don't know or care either," Piper reminded her. "Any time you're ready—"

She still knelt by the aquarium, watching the miniature world with keen, worried eyes. "Four of my fish gone in the last forty-eight hours," Miss Withers murmured. "A neon, a rosy tetra, a *betta*, and a *scalare*." She leaned even closer. Then she lifted the top of the tank, dipped her finger down into the water, and splashed.

Out from the shadows behind the red rock came a plump greenish-blue fish, wearing at the moment an extremely smug look upon its goggled, batrachian face. The female *betta* was very pleased with herself. Butter would not, as the old saying goes, melt in her mouth.

Neither would the long streamer, the antenna, which dangled from her jaws, vestigial remains of the missing angelfish. "Oscar, for heaven's sake," gasped the schoolteacher. "It was the *betta* all the time!"

He stood by the door, beckoning gently. "Oh, very well, Oscar. Since you have to be so official. It's a shame, though, that you don't share my interest in tropical fish. Sometimes we can learn the more interesting and valuable lessons from a close study of wild life. 'Sermons in stones,' you know." She turned out the light and picked up her bag. Then a sudden thought struck her and, murmuring something about her toothbrush, she disappeared into the bathroom.

Carefully locking the door behind her, she took out a packet of letters—love letters which should never have been written and which even now should not fall into the hands of the police or the district attorney. Swiftly she crumpled them, envelopes and all, into the bowl and touched a match to the lot. As they flared up she turned to open the window, not wanting the inspector in the other room to catch the sour, acrid scent of burning paper.

She turned back to the conflagration, stirring the burning letters with her finger so that nothing would be left but ashes. Then the schoolteacher caught her breath, for between the heavily written lines of Pat Montague's letters there had begun to appear faint gray writing—writing in another hand, a dainty, feminine hand. She caught the phrase "happy and sad at the same time" and again: "Oh, how could you say that …" and "… if you'll only wait and be patient …"

Tardily she splashed water from the faucet on the sodden mass, but it was no use. Miss Withers stood there, deep in thought, until she heard the inspector's impatient voice from the front room. Then she disposed of the ashes, washed her hands, and hurried out.

Meekly she followed the inspector out to the police car which waited at the hotel entrance and climbed into the rear seat. She did not have to be told how wide was the rift between them and how far she had fallen from Oscar Piper's good graces when she saw him close the door behind her and climb in front beside the driver.

"At any rate," she began pleasantly, "it appears that today will see the end of all this."

"It'll see the end of it for you," the inspector told her, and the roar of the motor as they jerked away from the curb put an end to further conversation.

In spite of all her delaying, they arrived at the Shoreham police station well ahead of time. None of the suspects had as yet arrived, and the inspector took her into the sheriff's vacant office and told her to wait.

"You stay here, and don't make a try to get away," he said.

"Never fear," Miss Withers told him. "I wouldn't miss this for the world." Then she caught his arm. "Oscar, for old time's sake, do me just one favor. I believe you said that all the suspects are to be here at seven?"

He nodded.

"Are they to be escorted down in police cars, as I was?"

"As it happens, no. They're all driving their own cars down so they can go right home afterwards, if and when they're cleared."

She told him what she wanted. "It would only take your men a minute—"

"This was no ordinary hit-run case," he pointed out.

"I know," she said. "But please have someone check their cars, anyway, very carefully. Especially the windshields!" He was obviously about to say "No" to her plan, so she added quickly: "If you'll agree to that, I'll tell you where to find Pat Montague."

That got him. "What? Where?"

"Relax, Oscar, I didn't hide him anywhere. But just think where you'd go if you just got out of jail, a dirty, smelly jail like this one, no doubt bug-infested and everything. You'd look for a bath, wouldn't you? Well, I happen to remember that there's a Turkish bath only halfway down the block, and I believe that customers in such places are allowed to have a bed for the night. "

For the first time that morning the inspector's face relaxed its grimness a little. "It's a deal," he told her, and went out.

Miss Withers was displeased but not surprised to hear the click of a key in the door. She sat down at the sheriff's desk, took out a pocket mirror from her handbag, and readjusted her hair and hat. Then she sat back patiently to wait. It was a wait of only a moment or two, for the telephone began to ring. Without hesitation she answered it.

"Is Vinge there? Dr. Farney speaking."

The schoolteacher buttoned down her conscience and answered with a businesslike voice, "He's tied up right now Doctor, but—"

"I was just going to tell him that I'd finished the post-mortem. But I'll bring my report over."

"The sheriff says that he'd like you to give me the details," she said hastily.

There was no sound at all at the other end of the line for as long as a count of ten in the prize-ring. Then Dr. Farney laughed. "That's funny," he chortled. "Because the sheriff just walked in here."

Miss Withers hung up just in time. For the door was being unlocked again. The inspector came in, looking glum. "Well, Oscar?"

"I looked at the suspects' cars," he said. "Especially the windshields. Why, will you tell me?"

"It's very simple," she said. "I've been riding around in taxicabs on these country roads in the evening enough to notice that at speeds of sixty and over the windshields become covered with dead bugs. At slower speeds the bugs slide up over the top. The murderer of Joe Searles must have been nervous and in a hurry, at least after the deed was done. So if you'll tell me whose windshield was a bug graveyard, I'll tell you—"

"Forget it," Piper said. "None of them showed more than a few dead bugs, and none of them had been recently cleaned, either. Come on, the investigation is about to begin."

"It'll be a complete waste of time," Miss Withers told him firmly. But she followed him down the hall. It appeared that the impending inquisition was to be held in the magistrate's room at the rear of the building. Sergeant Fischer, his arms folded, stood guard at the doorway, but he only nodded brusquely towards a seat in answer to her pleasant "Good morning." She plumped herself down in one of the very front pews and turned back to survey her fellow sufferers. She would have enjoyed calling the inspector's attention to one or two items, but he had hurried out again.

A majority of the official suspects in this case were already here, perched on hard folding chairs in the blaze of the summer sunshine which poured in through the high eastern windows. Commander Bennington had missed his morning shave, and beside him his wife was pale beneath a suntan makeup. Over in a corner Dr. Radebaugh sucked on an empty pipe, near where the Beales were sitting arm in arm.

Farther to the front Mame Boad was fanning herself with a folded newspaper, her shoes slipped off for greater comfort. Jed Nicolet was beside her, his fox face wary and alert. In the front of the room, on the other side of a wooden railing, stood a tall, curly-haired, cadaverous young man who must be Loomis, the district attorney. A court reporter was beside him, indicating that this was serious.

The inspector reentered, avoiding Miss Withers's beckoning gesture. He hurried through the barrier to confer with the district attorney.

Loomis glowered and then suddenly pulled out his watch and demanded loudly, "Well, what's keeping them? Get on the phone—"

Then there was a commotion in the hallway and all eyes turned to see Officer Lunnery enter very importantly with Thurlow Abbott in tow. The ex-matinee idol's eyes were heavy and bloodshot, but he seemed to perk up and draw himself together like the old campaigner he was as he made his entrance.

"Where are the others?" Piper demanded of the officer.

Lunnery hesitated. "Well, you see, it's like this—"

"My daughter Helen is not at home," Abbott interrupted in his froglike croak. "So she didn't receive the summons to appear here. She didn't even come home last night."

"And why not?" Loomis barked.

"I don't know. You see, we were expecting someone, a lawyer from Chicago, to arrive at nine-thirty, only he didn't say which airport or which line. So Helen took the sedan and went to La Guardia—I mean New York airport—and I took the roadster and went over to Newark, just in case. But I had the trip for nothing, because Mr. Malone arrived, I understand, at La Guardia, and Helen brought him here and delivered him. A short time later she disappeared, and I'm very worried about her."

"I'm not," said Miss Withers to nobody in particular.

"Okay," Piper said, taking the play away from the D.A. for the moment. "What about the other daughter?"

Thurlow Abbott shrugged expressively. "My daughter Lawn is locked in her room. She said that she's expecting a telephone call and that she doesn't feel like coming down right now. She says that if you want her you can swear out a warrant and serve it, and arrest her—"

"She said a lot more than that," chimed in Officer Lunney, "through the locked door."

"Good for her," observed Miss Withers, who had always wanted to see somebody call the police bluff on one of these so-called voluntary questionings. Let the minions of the law conform to the letter of the law, she always said.

The inspector seemed unperturbed. "I don't think that matters very much," he pointed out to the district attorney. "We don't really need Miss Abbott because as it happens we have proof that she was at home talking on the telephone at the exact time this second crime must have been committed. The hotel desk confirms this time, too, which was two minutes of twelve." His glance fell momentarily upon Miss Withers, and then he turned back to the D.A. "Shall we go ahead, Mr. Loomis, or wait for the sheriff?"

"Your party," said the D.A. with a wave of his hand and a smile which indicated clearly that it might be somebody else's party at any moment.

The inspector leaned on the wooden rail, facing the audience. "I suppose all you people know why you're here," he opened bluntly. "Huntley Cairns was murdered last Saturday afternoon and Joseph Searles last night. In case the exact connection isn't clear, I'll call on Mr. Beale."

Midge Beale stood up, stiff and perspiring, and after some prompting he related basically the same story of his adventures at the cocktail party that he had already confessed to Miss Withers.

"Thank you," said the inspector. "I might add that we know what book it was that you people were so interested in and how it fits into the picture. Some of you may think that dog poisoning is grounds for murder, or that it makes killing into justifiable homicide. The law doesn't look at it that way. Last evening, an hour or two before Searles was killed, it was brought to your attention that Huntley Cairns couldn't have been the dog poisoner but that Searles could have—and probably was. I want to know the movements of each of you people for the time between your conference at the Bennington home and say one o'clock this morning—"

Miss Withers closed her eyes and tried to think, shutting out as much as possible the righteous voices which kept insisting that they had all gone directly home to bed from the Benningtons' last night. Which meant, as the inspector went on to point out very clearly, that none of them had an alibi worth a nickel. "Not," he went on, "that alibis mean much in a case like this one. Any more than do fingerprints. It's pretty clear that the killer wore gloves—"

"And it's absolutely clear that he wore size 8½-B shoes, isn't it?" Miss Withers chimed in softly.

That let the cat out of the bag. Also, in theory at least, it cleared everyone in the room. The men's shoes were all too large, the women's too small, to have fitted the footprint which the schoolteacher had immortalized in pancake flour.

Everyone relaxed—everyone but Miss Withers. And, of course, District Attorney Loomis, who was chafing at the bit.

"What about Pat Montague?" he inquired of the inspector. "I don't suppose he's been picked up yet? Slipped through your fingers, I suppose?"

Miss Withers started to smile and then saw the look on the inspector's face. "We traced Montague to a Turkish bath down the street," he admitted. "He checked in there last night, but the attendants are a little hazy on the time. The rubber thought it was around midnight, but he clammed up when he found out why we were asking. They're very clear, though, on the time Montague left, which was at six-twenty this morning. It is possible that somebody warned him, as he was seen in a telephone booth just before he left."

"Why, Oscar Piper!" Miss Withers gasped. "If you're insinuating that I—"

The inspector paid her no attention whatsoever. "We're doing out best to locate him, Mr. Loomis," he went on. "Since he's out on a writ, we'll have to go easy—"

"It seems to me that the police have done nothing but go easy on this entire case!" Loomis snapped. "If this is a sample of the way you metropolitan cops investigate a homicide, then"—he smiled a thin smile—"I think that from now on we can handle our own affairs."

"I'll say we can!" spoke up a cheerful voice from the door, and everyone turned to see Sheriff Vinge entering, a broad beaming smile on his face. "Sorry I'm late, gentlemen, but something came up that puts an entirely different complexion on this case!"

He strode forward, and in his wake was Dr. Farney, looking tired and important. They both went through the railing. "We may as well have all this right out in the open," Sheriff Vinge continued. "This is Dr. Farney, everybody. He just got through examining the body of Joe Searles." He turned towards the doctor. "Can you tell us the cause of death in ordinary layman's language?"

"Asphyxia—that means strangulation—caused by drowning."

"Just like Mr. Cairns died?"

"I didn't post Cairns. From what I hear from my medical colleague"— and here Dr. Farney nodded towards Radebaugh—"it was the same sort of thing. Only when Searles died he was under the influence of fourteen ounces or more of methyl alcohol, plus sixty grains of so of seconal."

"Translate for the folks, Doctor?" Vinge asked.

"It is supposed to be a safer form of veronal and is sold on prescription only in this state. It's a sleeping powder, one of the barbiturates. The taste is bitter, and so it's usually given in capsules. Searles's liver showed 254 milligrams of barbital under Fabre's test. Not enough to poison the man, even tied up with the alcohol, which usually heightens the effect of the barbiturates, but enough to make him pretty dopey. His blood showed a good three hundredths of one per cent alcohol."

"Which means he was drunk, doesn't it, like you thought last night?" Sheriff Vinge was enjoying all this.

Farney nodded gravely. "He was very drunk."

"Question," said the inspector. "Any chance he could have taken the seconal to make him sleep?"

"The usual dose, and Dr. Radebaugh will bear me out, is one five-grain capsule. He had twelve times that in him."

Sheriff Vinge nodded. "Thank you, Doctor. Please sit down, we may need you later." He turned to the inspector and the D.A. "Now, gentlemen, I'm going to lay it on the line. The suggestion was made by somebody else last night, and at the time I didn't pay much attention. Guess I owe somebody an apology. ..." He nodded towards Miss Withers, who sat up stiffly and blinked.

"Yes, sir," Sheriff Vinge continued. "It's been proved to my satisfaction that Joe Searles was the dog poisoner that ran riot around here a while ago. Looks to me like Huntley Cairns got wise to it—maybe from that same book in his library that upset you folks so much—and he let on to Searles that he knew. And so the old man up and drowned him in his own pool, maybe using a couple of garden rakes tied or fastened together—"

Somebody in the room let go with a long, heartfelt sigh, but Miss Withers couldn't tell who it was. She sat stiffly on the edge of her seat and wondered what was coming next.

"Joe Searles thought he had got by with it, and he did his best to pin it on a young man who came in on the scene just after he'd finished murdering his employer. But his conscience was worrying him. He knew that the case against Montague was collapsing and that he himself was next in line. He was a proud old goat—his folks were once big shots around here, and he didn't intend to be tried and executed for murder. So day before yesterday he went down to the hardware store and bought him an old .38 revolver—"

"But there wasn't any gun in his cottage!" Miss Withers burst in.

Sheriff Vinge bowed politely. "Right, ma'am. He prob'y threw it in the Sound. Blowing out your brains is a hard way to go. Besides, he musta felt that he owed it to society to go the same way he sent Cairns. So he got hold of a bottle of sleeping powders, poured 'em into some whiskey, and tossed off the mixture so he wouldn't feel any pain. Then he got a pail of water, balanced himself on the edge of his couch, and shoved himself in!"

The silence in the room was so thick it could have been sliced, Miss Withers thought, with a butter knife.

"Dr. Farney admits," the sheriff continued, "that death could have been accidental or suicidal. Men have drowned themselves in bathtubs and in shallow streams."

The doctor, seated close beside Sheriff Vinge, looked up and nodded gravely. "Possible," he said. "Quite possible."

"I can believe any number of impossible things before breakfast," murmured Miss Withers. "But not that."

"And that ain't all!" continued Vinge. "Like the doctor told you, seconal can be traced because it's sold on a prescription. Well, the only bottle of the stuff sold in Shoreham in six months was on a prescription by somebody in this room—"

Dr. Harry Radebaugh stood up, smiling nervously. "I'll admit that I signed that prescription," he admitted. "But it wasn't for Searles, who was no patient of mine. It was for Mr. Thurlow Abbott!"

Abbot said something, his voice hardly more than a whisper, but it was Sheriff Vinge who took the floor. "We know that," he said. "It's on the records down to the drugstore. But remember that Joe Searles had the run of the Cairns house, and he could easy enough have gone up to Mr. Abbott's bathroom and borrowed the sleeping pills."

Dr. Radebaugh sat down again. Thurlow Abbott took a deep breath and tried to speak, but this time it was the district attorney who drowned out his feeble effort. "Then," Loomis said, "you're satisfied, Sheriff, that the whole thing can be written off as murder and suicide?"

Vinge nodded. "I'm not sorry to save Knight's County the expense of further investigation and a big expensive murder trial." He turned to the crowd. "Folks, I'm sorry you all had to be dragged out of bed at this hour and brought down here. But we had to investigate every possible lead and eliminate everything we could. You can all go now." He turned to the inspector and held out his hand. "Thanks, Mr. Piper, for your help. Guess we all have our off days." He turned his head. "I really should be thanking that schoolteacher friend of yours because she sort of accidentally put us on the right track."

But Miss Withers was not waiting for congratulations. She had caught Midge and Adele Beale as they went out of the door. "I'm so happy to see you two young people reunited," she said.

"Sure." Midge grinned.

"There was no reason to quarrel just because Huntley Cairns gave your wife a pension, was there?"

Adele blinked. "What? Oh, you know about that? Well, it wasn't as simple as that. It was just that I was responsible for inspiring Huntley's business. You see, years ago when we were going around together, we heard Thurlow Abbott complaining one night about his lack of luck in getting back on the stage. He was wishing that his public would write letters to the producers demanding his return, and half-kiddingly I said that we ought to get together and write a thousand or so, signing any old name. Huntley seized on that right away. It didn't work for Mr. Abbott, because his voice was really gone, but it worked for other people in show business."

"And Mr. Cairns was grateful to you? It sheds a new light on his character."

"He was scared," Adele corrected. "He didn't want me to let the secret out. There's millions in it. Why only recently Huntley started in on Congress. You see, congressmen love to be photographed beside a great pile of letters, supposedly from the voters back home, upholding their filibuster on the Fair Employment Practices Act, or their stand on abolishing the OPA, or whatever. Anyhow, Huntley paid me twenty-five a week to keep quiet." She smiled. "You see?"

"I do indeed," said Miss Withers. She beamed at them as they hurried out of the place and inwardly wished that she could somehow unite a certain other young couple as Midge and his Adele were united.

The schoolteacher waited patiently in the hallway until at last the inspector came out, his shoulders sagging. "Go ahead and crow," he told her bitterly.

"Don't be silly," she snapped. "Hens don't crow. They cackle when they've laid an egg, but this time the egg was laid by the sheriff—"

"I'm afraid not," Piper told her. "The whole thing's washed up, anyway."

"Is it?"

"For me, at least." He went on, and she fell into step beside him.

"Oscar, didn't you notice a few minutes ago that Thurlow Abbott was trying to say something? Nobody gave him a chance—but I stopped him in the hall, and I listened. What if he's telling the truth and that bottle of sleeping powders is still in his medicine cabinet at home?"

CHAPTER FIFTEEN

"You once accused me," Miss Withers reminded the inspector, "of being a self-appointed gadfly to the police. This is one time, I warn you, when I intend to admit the soft impeachment. Oscar, this case is not settled, and you know it! In spite of Sheriff Vinge's neat little house of cards. He's only trying to get out of it the easy way, without stepping on anybody's toes. Don't you see? His theory leaves too many things unaccounted for."

"Such as?" Piper yawned widely.

"The footprint, for one thing."

Piper nodded wearily. "We talked about that. It's his theory that it was your own footprint, and that the pancake flour you dumped on it moistened around the edges for a little way—enough to add a few sizes."

She sniffed. "Of course he didn't test it? I thought not. Besides, what about the missing bottle from which Searles drank his whiskey cut with sleeping powders? What about the missing revolver?"

"All right, all right. But what can I do? I'm off the case."

"Officially?"

"It amounts to that. I suppose Vinge will phone the commissioner that they have no further need for me, and I'll be ordered to report back to my desk at Centre Street."

"But you haven't been so ordered, have you?"

The inspector admitted that he hadn't. "Well, then!" Miss Withers sniffed. "And am I still in technical custody?"

He shook his head. "That was Loomis's idea in the beginning. He asked me to apologize to you."

"And well he might! Mr. District Attorney Loomis will be apologizing to both of us before this day is through. Oscar, will you take me up to the Cairns house right now?"

He shook his head. "No, definitely no. Look, I didn't get a wink of sleep last night, and I'm out on my feet, and I don't give a hoot in hell—"

Ten minutes later they were being driven out of town in a police sedan, the inspector dispiritedly huddled in the front seat beside the driver, and Miss Withers chatting away happily in back. "Murder will out, Oscar," she told him. "Sometimes it needs help, that's all. It's really too bad that you don't care for tropical fish, or you might see what I have in mind. But forget the fish. Has it ever occurred to you that we are often amply repaid by a study of *dogs* and what happens to them?"

"I suppose so," Piper grunted noncommittally. He turned to the uniformed driver. "Kick it up."

The car lurched ahead. "As a matter of fact," continued the schoolteacher, "even the proverbs about dogs are interesting. There is the lovely Mexican one about 'he who lies down with dogs gets up with fleas,' and then there's 'a dog's life,' as though most dogs did not live a very carefree and enviable existence indeed, except, of course, the dog's unfortunate enough to live in the neighborhood of Shoreham. They also say that 'every dog has his day,' though of course it is usually a night, instead—"

The inspector leaned over and hit the siren a short blast to give them the right of way at an intersection. When the din ceased Miss Withers's voice was blithely continuing: "But as a matter of fact, I have recently come to the conclusion that 'give a dog a bad name' is the most apt of all our proverbs about our four-footed friends."

With a wild gleam in his eye the inspector hit the siren and kept it going, so that they raced through the early morning streets of Shoreham village at sixty miles an hour, accompanied by a wailing as of all the devils of hell.

They found the Cairns house shuttered and silent, but after a couple of rings at the doorbell Thurlow Abbott appeared, still chewing on his morning toast. "If you're looking for my daughter Helen, she still isn't home," he announced.

Miss Withers spoke up to say that they had hardly expected to find

Mrs. Cairns at home. "The inspector and I only wanted a look at your bathroom," she informed him.

"The bathroom?" Abbott blinked, and then his face brightened. "Oh, the sleeping powders! It's just as I said, the bottle is there. Why, I even took a capsule last night!"

Miss Withers nudged the inspector, feeling somewhat triumphant. They followed Thurlow Abbott across the long drawing room and up the stairs and at last were led into the small but luxurious bath which opened off the hall and also into his room. "There!" he croaked. "There were fifty capsules originally. I've taken two or three."

For the first time the inspector began to take an interest in what was going on. "We may have something here," after all!"

But Miss Withers was counting them. "Forty-seven," she totaled with a certain satisfaction. Then she peered at the label, which had been filled out in neat typescript by the druggist: "Mr. Thurlow Abbott—May 12—Dr. Radebaugh," plus a key number.

"I think this ought to be Exhibit A or something," she told the inspector as she slipped the bottle into her handbag.

"Let's get going," he urged. "I'm anxious to toss that bottle into Sheriff Vinge's fat face, and then—"

"Softly, Oscar, softly," Miss Withers said. "We have a trump card in our hand, sure enough. But we need something more. While we're here"—she turned to Abbott—"can you tell us if any one in this house made a telephone call early this morning?"

He frowned and shook his head. "At least not until after I left for the police station with Officer Lunney. But we can ask the servants."

They went back downstairs again. In the kitchen both Jeff and Beulah insisted that to the best of their knowledge and belief nobody had called out at all that day.

"But the phone rang and rang, though," Beulah suddenly put in. "It was a few minutes after six, and we weren't even up yet. It stopped ringing before I could slip something on and—"

"You mean, whoever was calling hung up? Or was it answered?" Miss Withers was impatient.

"I guess they hung up. Nobody was home but Miss Lawn, and like I told you, she's been locked in her room in a temper since before dinnertime last night."

Miss Withers nodded. "Yes, Oscar. A family disagreement, I believe."

"My daughter Lawn," Thurlow Abbott put in, "has a most violent temper. A very perverse girl, all her life—she just won't pull her oar in time with the rest. She was annoyed last night because Helen and I were using both cars."

"Did she know what you were using them for?" the schoolteacher put in.

He shook his head. "Helen didn't see any point in telling her. At any rate, Lawn blew up as usual. When she is in a temper she has a way of locking herself in her room and playing symphony music full blast."

Jeff and Beulah both nodded. "That's just how it was last night, from eight o'clock until well after midnight. She played a lot of Rachmaninoff," Jeff said.

"And Debussy," his wife added.

"And Shostakovitch's Fifth and Eighth, over and over again. Then she suddenly switched to an old record of the suicide song, and she played that until we thought we'd have to put cotton in our ears."

"What suicide song?" the inspector demanded.

"Lawn," said Thurlow Abbott, "has a recording of 'Gloomy Sunday,' the song that was supposed to have started a wave of suicides in Vienna before the war. When I got home last night, after waiting out at the Newark airport until after midnight, she had it on full blast. That's why I had to take a sleeping powder to get any rest."

"The poor girl," Miss Withers was murmuring in an absent tone. For a moment or two she had withdrawn from the conversation, busy with something in her handbag. She turned suddenly to Thurlow Abbott. "By the way, did the sleeping pill do its work? I mean, did you go directly to sleep?"

He nodded, obviously surprised.

"How very odd," the schoolteacher observed. "Well, Oscar, we seem to have done everything here that can be done. Thank you very much, Mr. Abbott, for your help. Please go on with your breakfast, we can see ourselves out."

But he followed them part of the way. "I'm really worried," he said. "About Helen—"

"She'll turn up," the inspector said confidently.

"And anyway," Miss Withers pointed out, "Helen is of age, and she's chosen her own path. If I may make a suggestion, there is someone else who needs you more right now." She looked towards the upper floor.

Abbott smiled. "You mean Lawn? She's sufficient unto herself."

"I wonder," said Miss Withers softly. "I wonder if any of us is ever that sufficient?" She took the inspector's arm and led him out of the place, a very much happier man than he had been only half an hour before.

But they paused in the front doorway. "Maybe I ought to use the phone," he suggested, "to order a broadcast sent out to pick up Helen Cairns? Or Pat Montague?"

The schoolteacher shook her head. "I'm not so sure, Oscar. Things are moving a little too fast for me."

Then he grinned, himself again. "Don't be so mysterious. I know why you asked Abbott if the sleeping pill worked. You wanted to find out if, without his knowing it, maybe Helen came back here last night after he was asleep and maybe made or answered a phone call this morning."

"Something like that, but not quite," she confessed. "You see, Oscar, I made a little experiment. It's very odd about Thurlow Abbott's getting to sleep so quickly last night. Because I tasted two of those sleeping capsules, and they're filled with common baking soda!"

The inspector's shoulders sagged again. "Judas Priest in a bathtub!" he moaned.

Miss Withers stared at him rather queerly. "We still have a trump," she pointed out. "Even if we have to refill this bottle with genuine capsules. Because Sheriff Vinge is wrong, and we both know he is wrong."

"He probably knows he's wrong too," Piper said. "But knowing it and admitting it are two different things."

She nodded without listening. "You know, Oscar, it's a shame that your men didn't get to the Turkish bath soon enough to catch Pat Montague and find out just what shoe size he wears."

The inspector looked at her blankly. "You're not starting to suspect him, after sticking up for him all this time?"

"Of course," she continued, "it just occurred to me that we might determine his size from other sources."

"You mean the Army? They're great on detail, but I doubt if they keep a record of the shoe size of every first lieutenant."

"I didn't mean that. I meant—well, didn't Pat Montague, by his own admission, take a walk from the highway over there down through the lawns and flower gardens to the swimming pool? That was only last Saturday, and there's only been a sprinkle of rain since then."

"Sure enough. I should have remembered. Come on."

"If you don't mind, I'll let you do the leg work," said Miss Withers. She watched while he hurried off and then pushed in against the front door, which she had never quite allowed to close during their conversation.

Once inside, she listened for a moment. There was no sound in the house except the clatter of Thurlow Abbott's coffee cup in the dining room. She went swiftly and silently across the drawing room, up the stairs, and along the hall, to tap gently with her fingernail upon a certain door.

There was no sound from within. "Lawn!" whispered Miss Withers, and then tapped again.

"Oh, go away!" came a voice from within, a voice with a sob in it.

"It's I—Miss Withers. I'll go, but first I have important news for you."

The lock clicked, and the door opened to disclose Lawn Abbott in black silk pajamas, her eyes red-rimmed. "I don't much care what news you have," the girl said. "He's really gone—to reenlist in the Army!"

Miss Withers nodded wisely. "So that's what he called up to tell you this morning! Still, there might be ways to prevent him from taking that step."

"It's no use, I tell you!" The girl shook her head so furiously that the long dark hair whipped her face.

"If I may say so," the schoolteacher said gently, "your greatest mistake has been your insistence on playing a lone hand. You have friends—you have always had friends, no doubt, who would have been glad to help you if you'd let them."

Lawn flickered a thin bitter smile. "Well, perhaps. But it's too late now."

"Is it? I wonder. Offhand I can think of a number of ways of bringing Pat Montague back, still in civilian clothes. And I don't mean under arrest, either."

The girl waited, statuelike, her lips parted.

"I can't say any more now," continued Miss Withers. "I'm not even supposed to be here. But I'll make you a promise. If you'll be at my cottage at noon there'll be somebody waiting there who wants to see you more than anybody in the world."

Lawn Abbott automatically gnawed at the nail of her right forefinger. "I don't believe you," she said tonelessly.

"Or somebody who will want to see you," the schoolteacher corrected herself, "by that time. He'll be waiting there at noon, remember. I've got to run now, before the inspector misses me."

She turned and hurried out of the place, her heart pounding. As luck would have it, the inspector was just returning from his search of the grounds, a wry smile on his face. "What luck, Oscar?" she hailed him.

"Don't quite know. I found the tracks all right, where Pat Montague stumbled through a soft flowerbed. His print is just the size of mine, and I wear a nine. Do you suppose your flour *moulage* could be off half a size? That's less than a quarter of an inch."

"Perhaps," she said. "It could be tested, I suppose. But that can wait. Oscar, where is Camp Nivens located?"

"The Army separation center?" He thought. "It's out beyond Garden City. Why?"

"How long would it take to get there from here?"

"No more than an hour, certainly, by auto. Three times that long by train, because you'd have to go all the way into Penn Station and change."

Miss Withers looked pleased. "Then it's going to be more simple than I thought. Oscar, I wish you'd get the Garden City police on the phone."

"But why?"

She shook her head. "I told you this was the last day on the case," she reminded him. "If you'll do what I ask, I'll make it the last half-day."

The inspector held the car door open for her, but this time he climbed into the back seat beside her. "I don't know what you're up to, exactly," he admitted. "But you're acting as if you knew something."

She nodded. "I think I do, Oscar. I think I've known for some time, but a lot of possibilities had to be eliminated first. As a matter of fact, I've dropped hints enough so you ought to know too. But please let me play it my way. It's easier to demonstrate than explain, and besides, there are some holes big enough to drive a truck through in my hypothesis." She went on to explain just what it was that she wanted him to say to the Garden City police.

The inspector nearly fell out of the car. "What earthly good will it do," he demanded, "to locate Pat Montague and to run down Helen Cairns and to tell them that the case is all solved when it isn't?"

"Sheriff Vinge says it is," she reminded him. "Besides, the important thing is to have a report on what Pat and Helen do afterwards." There was a reassuring ring of confidence in her voice.

She was to regret that confidence, and very soon. The inspector dropped her off at the hotel, promising to reappear later on when he had attended to all the things that needed attending, and she forced herself to make breakfast. But there was nothing of it except the coffee which attracted her, and she drank that clear and black. Her hand, she knew, was full of the top honors, all the face cards. But suppose, as in the old story about the man who played cards on an ocean liner with the devil, her adversary should choose to lead out the green ace of Hippogriffs?

Miss Withers turned on the fluorescent light above her tank of tropical fish and noticed that the leaves of the aquatic plants were turning yellow along the edges and that the water was roiled and cloudy. She shrugged and then crossed the room to seat herself on a hard chair, with—as she would have expressed it—one eye on the door and one on the telephone.

Miss Hildegarde Withers was still sitting there, in almost the same position, when finally there came the sound of quick, nervous steps along the path and a sharp tat-a-tat-tat on the door. She opened it hastily and saw that Lawn Abbott stood there—a strange, new Lawn. The dark circles were gone from around her eyes, and her mouth looked softer. She was flushed and breathless, almost as if she had run all the way.

"Is he here?" she cried.

The schoolteacher indicated the clock. "You're a little early, child," she pointed out.

Lawn slapped her silver-mounted crop against her riding-breeches. "I'd have been earlier yet if my father hadn't gone off somewhere in the little car. And of course Helen is still using the sedan. So I had to saddle up that big hack of mine and ride down—it's not much more than a mile along the beach. I hope the hotel people won't mind; I tied him to a clothesline out back."

"Do sit down," invited Miss Withers, indicating the divan.

But Lawn Abbott was in a prowling mood. "Tell me," she begged. "You've heard from Pat? He'll really be here?"

"Be patient, young lady. I made you a promise, didn't I? I'm glad you came early, though, because we have a lot to talk about. We may as well have our chat over a nice cup of coffee, don't you think?" She started for the kitchen.

"None for me," Lawn said quickly. "I'm too excited." She hesitated. "I need something all right. You haven't—no, I don't suppose you'd have a drink in the house?"

Miss Withers blinked. "You mean you'd like a slug in it, as the inspector so inelegantly says? I'll see if I can't arrange it." She turned the burner on under the coffee pot and then after a few minutes poured out two cups, but her mind was elsewhere. Out in the living room Lawn was pacing up and down like a bear in a cage.

"I don't see why you're taking all this trouble," she was saying.

"You've never been an old maid," the schoolteacher advised her as she reached up to the top shelf to take down the half-pint bottle of cognac that had been purchased for her Thanksgiving plum pudding. She carefully poured a modicum into the cup that wasn't cracked. "There is, you know, a certain pleasure in straightening out people's lives—in a way it's being *Dea ex Machina*—"

"The what?"

"The Goddess from the Machine, who swoops down to make everything come right, at least in the classical theater." Miss Withers added, "I hope!" in a lower voice, and then let fall a few drops of the spirit into the other cup. She certainly needed some outside help if she was going to carry off the next half-hour successfully. After a moment's delay she finally entered the living room, bearing a tray which held, besides the two cups of coffee, a sugar bowl and cream pitcher. She put the tray down on the low table before the divan, wishing with all her heart that her visitor would light somewhere. She didn't want Lawn glancing into the dark corner behind the divan, at least not yet.

Coffee could hardly be drunk standing, that was one good thing. Lawn dropped down on the cushions as she accepted her cup. She accepted it and made a wry face.

"Isn't it all right?" Miss Withers asked quickly. "Perhaps the slug was too strong—I never use alcohol myself—"

"Oh, it's okay," Lawn said, drinking deeply.

Miss Withers took her own cup and retreated across the room. She took a sip and decided that while some people might like coffee with brandy she would have it plain for the rest of her life. "It's too bad," she began pleasantly, "that you didn't come down to the open house at the police station this morning." She sipped again. "The whole mystery was solved, you know."

Lawn's cup clattered in the saucer. "What did you say?"

"It was *solved*. The investigation is over. Sheriff Vinge decided that Searles murdered your brother-in-law and then killed himself when he thought he was going to be caught."

"You don't believe that!"

Miss Withers cocked her head. "The sheriff was very, very convincing. After all, I'm only an amateur."

Lawn sat up straight. "Look here, Miss Withers, I want a showdown. You've been very nice to me from the beginning. But I've got to know where I stand. I've got to know what you're driving at!"

"Yes?" To gain a little time Miss Withers finished her coffee. "What do you want to know?"

"Everything! But first I want to know where my sister Helen was all last night and where she is now."

There was a long pause. "I have my own opinion as to her whereabouts last night, but it's only a guess. As to her present whereabouts, I think that she might be on her way here."

"Oh!" Lawn said. She took up her cup and thoughtfully drank the remainder. Miss Withers heaved a great sigh of relief. She looked at the clock, wondering how long it was before betapentalin took effect. It shouldn't be so very long, she decided, especially since she had used half the bottle.

"It's nearly twelve," she observed.

"It's time Pat was here, if he's coming," Lawn said. "What happened to make him change his mind?"

"He simply sees things more clearly by this time, or I hope he does. You've waited for Pat Montague a long time, haven't you?"

"That's no secret. I wanted him since the first day I saw him. And then I had to stand back and watch my sister put her lovely tentacles around and around him, strangling him—" She laughed without humor. "That was why I ran away from home," Lawn went on. "The time I told you about. Helen and Pat got engaged, and I couldn't stand it. She could have had anybody, anybody at all, and there was nobody but Pat for me. He belonged to me, don't you see?"

All of a sudden Miss Hildegarde Withers felt supremely confident. It must, she thought, have been the few drops of brandy that she let fall into her cup out in the kitchen. Her cup—the cracked one.

Just to reassure herself, she turned the cup around, but the brandy had made everything fuzzy so that she couldn't even focus her eyes on the crack. Even so, everything was going swimmingly. "You know," she confessed, "there was a time when I thought that you yourself might be the murderer of Huntley Cairns."

Lawn smiled at that, but she bit at her fingernail again. "Why in the world did you think that?"

Miss Withers reminded herself that she must be very careful and yet daring too. Then her lips opened of their own volition. "It was because you didn't have any alibi. Your horse couldn't come into court and say what time it was that you brought him in from your ride on Saturday afternoon. Who could say whether you came up the hill to the swimming pool after Huntley Cairns was killed or before?"

"Go on," Lawn begged. "I hadn't realized I was that much of a suspect."

"I suspected Helen too. Because she spilled cocktails on her dress at the party and was gone a long time while she was supposed to be changing. She could have gone out for a swim, possibly wanting to keep away from her guests until she had regained her composure. She could have been swimming in the pool when Cairns came down for his dip—she could even have pretended a cramp while he was undressing, and when he rushed out to save her she could have pulled him in and drowned him. He was a very poor swimmer, and both you and your sister were brought up in the water, like most of the young people along the Shore."

"I can't believe it!" Lawn whispered. She was crouched back on the divan now, looking smaller, more withdrawn.

"Neither could I, my child. Then it occurred to me that it might have been you in Helen's bathing suit, which she'd left in the dressing room." Miss Withers felt happy and glowing and a little careless. Most of all she wanted to talk and talk and talk. "At any rate, it wouldn't have been difficult for a good swimmer to pull Cairns down to the bottom of the pool and hook his clothing on to that jagged bit of metal so he'd stay down and probably not be found until the next morning."

"Go on, keep talking!" Lawn demanded.

"Oh, I shall. But just between us both, I'll admit that this is the last time I'll have coffee with brandy; it seems to have affected my tongue just a teeny bit. Where was I? Oh, yes, about what happened next—or what could have happened. You slipped out of the pool and into the dressing-room, and to save time you put your riding clothes back on over the wet swimming suit. Outside, Pat Montague and Searles were discovering the body, so you sat tight with the door locked. Searles tricked Pat into going in the other dressing room to phone and locked him in before he rushed to the house to telephone—and you came out and let him go free."

Lawn was stiff and frozen, but she still showed no desire to do any confessing, which the schoolteacher thought was very odd. The girl said, "Pat doesn't believe any of this pipe dream, does he?"

"I wouldn't know. But at the time he was fooled by the white bathing suit. And by the moisture which came through your riding breeches from the bathing suit—he thought you had brought your horse in all lathered up, which was contrary to your usual practice. Of course, neither he nor anybody else saw a motive for you to kill Cairns."

Lawn smiled faintly. "That's right. Why would I get rid of him and leave Helen a free, wealthy widow?"

"That puzzled me too for a while," the schoolteacher confided. "Then I realized how much you wanted Pat Montague for yourself. You knew that the moment he came back your sister would rush into his arms. She even kept a bag packed with a few of her summer clothes, so that she could elope in a minute if he asked her. But you saw that if your sister were mixed up in a murder Pat wouldn't ask her!"

"And so?" the girl prompted.

"It really worked, didn't it? Huntley Cairns dead was an obstacle between the lovers that he would never have been living. Pat thought that Helen did it, and she thought that he did. Of course you never meant to have Pat walk in and become suspect number one, even though you knew he would show up soon. You'd received his phone calls meant for Helen, no doubt mimicking the maid. Did you pretend to take a message so he would think Helen didn't care enough to call back? I'm sure you did. I'm sure you intended the police to suspect Helen, too, because of the damp white bathing suit crammed down in her laundry bag. It was when I saw the suit that I began to feel you must be the murderer, only at that time I didn't see *how*."

Lawn sat there, stiff and silent. "You see, you're what the medical profession calls an 'onychophagist,' or 'eater of fingernails.' And the laces of Helen's suit were ripped instead of untied—and a person without fingernails has a good deal of difficulty in untying anything, especially when in a hurry." Miss Withers swayed in her chair, but her voice went steadily, monotonously on. "Pat's inept arrival on the scene rather spoiled your original idea of involving Helen. And then of course we were all confused by the red herring across the trail—I mean the local committee who were trying to run down the dog poisoner. I wasted a good deal of time on them, and you of course encouraged that, since it took suspicion off yourself and off Pat." The schoolteacher shook her head sharply. "Have you noticed that this room is going round and round like a carousel?"

The girl didn't answer, and Miss Withers picked up her coffee cup again, studying it most carefully. The crack must be somewhere, unless she was losing her eyesight.

Across the room Lawn Abbott had one fist in the pocket of her tweed riding jacket, a pocket which, Miss Withers remembered, had sagged heavily as the girl entered the room. "Don't stop now," Lawn prompted her in a voice that was low and hoarse.

Miss Withers knew that she couldn't stop, though she tried to put on the brakes. The words kept pouring out like water from a leaky faucet. "I don't mind telling you," she heard herself saying, "that in spite of my suspicions I never really began to understand the setup until Searles was murdered. By that time both you and Helen were very worried about Pat. He was in jail, and it looked as if the police meant to hold him and try to convict him. You both took steps—Helen sent for a clever lawyer with a reputation of saving lost causes. But you realized that if another murder, done in the same general fashion, happened while Pat was locked up, it would clear him completely. You heard over the radio that he had confessed—which he did in an effort to try to save Helen—and that clinched it—"

"Go on," Lawn said. "Go on and keep going."

Miss Withers leaned back in her chair. She was dizzy and she wanted to lie down and go to sleep, but she knew that she mustn't do that. There was something that had to come first, only she couldn't remember quite what it was. Something about a trap that had to be sprung.

"You picked Searles because he was one of the first on the murder scene and he might have noticed something. It was easy enough to give him a bottle of whiskey to take home last night. I don't know how you got down to his cottage—I imagine you rode your horse along the beach, as you rode here today. Your radio-phonograph is automatic and, like most automatics, it plays the last record over and over again until turned off. It would have been easy enough for you to step through your window on to the balcony, murder Searles, and get back to turn the machine off before the needle wore out. You didn't know that you had left a footprint in Searles's cottage, a size 8½-B footprint."

Lawn Abbott shook her head. "I don't wear that size, nor anything near it."

"Not in shoes, no. But riding boots are made several sizes larger than shoes, with a wide, heavy sole. It was you, of course, who shoved Searles's head into a pail of water—you must have been in the midst of that when you answered his phone at my call. It was really an excellent impersonation, though you only had to speak a word or two. But it was brilliant of you to phone me right back, as if from your home, giving yourself a perfect alibi! You took the whiskey bottle away with you because it would, of course, show traces of the sleeping powder you had borrowed from your father's bathroom, and you took the gun just in case it would come in handy later—such as now."

Lawn took her hand out of her pocket, and the pistol was gripped in it—not aimed, but just cradled easily.

"Tell me," she said quietly, "just why do you believe this nightmare you've dreamed up?"

"Because it makes sense," the schoolteacher whispered. Her lips were a little stiff and strange, as if they belonged to somebody else. "Because from the first it's been evident that you're an antisocial type. There's an old proverb—'Give a dog a bad name and he'll live up to it'—and that fitted you. You have a long-standing reputation for making your own rules."

"Thinking it and proving it are two different matters," the girl reminded her. The hands of the clock were now pointing to a few minutes after twelve, but it seemed to Miss Withers that she had been here for two lifetimes.

"There honestly wasn't much proof," the schoolteacher confided, still vainly fighting the heavy compulsion to unburden her mind of any and all secrets. "That's why I set this trap. That's why I had someone else listening, ready to arrest you at the right time after you'd confessed everything. You have confessed everything, haven't you? I rather think you must have, but everything is getting so foggy—"

She had to squint to see Lawn at all, and even then the girl looked like something seen through the wrong end of an opera glass. There was a long silence, broken only by Lawn Abbott's quick, irregular breathing and the pounding of Miss Withers's heart. No, there was another sound, a soft purring, which had been, she realized, going on for some time. ...

Lawn noticed it too. "What's that?" she cried.

It came again, a definite, unmistakable snore. Miss Withers fought a losing battle to keep silent and then heard her lips form the words: "Why, my dear, that's the inspector. I put him there, stretched out on a blanket, so he could overhear your confession. Remember what I said about somebody being here who wanted you? Well, he wants you, for murder—"

The girl whipped to her feet, Joe Searles's revolver gripped tight in her hand, and her face hardened into a death mask. Miss Withers tried to scream, but now that she really wanted to make a noise she found herself as mute as in a nightmare.

"I know she's going to lean over behind the divan and she's going to shoot Oscar Piper, the poor dear tired man, and I have to sit here and watch it all because I can't even stand up. ..." She tried manfully, but her legs refused to work. Then she fell sideways against the little table which held her coffee cup. There was the shuddering roar of an explosion somewhere inside her head, and the rush of many waters.

CHAPTER SIXTEEN

After forty days and forty nights the rushing waters quieted and finally began to recede, leaving the highest peak of Miss Hildegarde Withers's mind exposed to the clear cold air of consciousness. She was being heckled by a masculine voice which kept insisting, "Drink this, like a good girl."

Slowly she opened her eyes, saw that she was in her own bed and that Dr. Harry Radebaugh was leaning over her. It was dark outside, and the wind blew rain against the windowpane. "I will never again in my whole life drink anything but water," she murmured with an effort that left her weak. She closed her eyes again.

"But this will settle your stomach," the doctor insisted. He lifted her shoulders, holding the glass to her lips. Too weak to put up further resistance, she downed the bitter draught.

"Never you mind my stomach," she begged. "Just give me something to keep the top of my head from coming off!"

Dr. Radebaugh laughed. "You're going to be all right."

"Drop that cheerful bedside manner, young man. I know how awful I feel. I'm numb all over. Where did that vixen shoot me?"

"You're not shot, Hildegarde." It was the inspector's voice, and she opened her eyes again to stare at him coldly.

"Neither are you, I observe! Though you should have been, for going to sleep at the post!" She turned back towards the doctor. "Well, what have I got?"

"Just the damnedest hangover that anybody ever had," the medico told

158